The Murder of a Boss

a Boss

Rise of the Black Diamond Cartel

C@$INO DI@MOND$

Contents

ACKNOWLEDGEMENT

It can't be denied, and it must be said, had the haters not said I couldn't, I know I wouldn't. For those who were glad to see me fall, you are my motivation- the reason I write. You thought I would never be shit, but you inspired me to rise above, to leave you all behind to kiss my ass! I could name drop all you motherfuckas, but why give you publicity? You'll never get no shine off me! You know if you kept it real with me. Today I write because the art within must find an outlet- but it's an art based on my reality, one you all feared. I don't hold it against you- a person can only do what they are. You hated because you're haters. You thought I failed, but truth be told I've been set free to explore my best shit and share it with the world. No matter what, when I'm long gone, I'm leaving behind a legacy for my kids. When they grow up to be adults, they'll never get another man rich from their labors. Because their father owns K@SH HOUSE PUBLICATIONS. That's right haters, I own 100% of everything that I write, and even if I don't write, I still get paid! Thanks to all my haters!) Question...What will your family have when you leave this world? A funeral, a headstone, a picture and debt. Oh, and one less hater! Also remember, hatin' don't pay. For all of my people in the slums with dreams, don't let the haters choke you out. Separate and rise above and leave your mark on this world. To all my readers around the world who have purchased this book, I want you to know that I really appreciate you and I promise to go harder in every book. To all my readers on lock, and all my niggas in the Robertson unit, keep yo' head up and yo' ass down! True Story. K@SH HOUSE about to take it to another level. Enjoy this story.

C@SINO DI@MOND$

DEDICATION

I would like to give thanks to my Greater because without him I wouldn't have been able to accomplish everything that I have accomplished.

To my wonderful mother, Brenda Clark...I wish you were here to see that I finally made it. I'm finally doing something positive with my life. I know you're smiling down on me right now saying, 'You could've been doing this! Yeah, I know it took a while for me to open my eyes. But I'm seeing everything that you saw in me and I promise to stay focused and represent you every time I step out! I love you Momma. Rest in peace...

To my father Phillip Clark: Man thanks for being a great dad, you always took care of your business and made sure I understood what being a man was all about. Thanks for always loving my mother, and keeping it 1,000 with me at all times. Just chill and be still, I'mma send some love your way.

To my brother Aundre Lewis: It's crazy how we been ridin' this time together on the same unit. You really opened my eyes to a lot of shit and I thank you for all the ideas you forced me to steal from you to make this book flow like it does. Lol I Love you nigga.

To my bro Twilley: Nigga, you always been 1,000 with me. I remember when I met you, I was 16 years old. The youngest nigga at the Kappa with you. You always treated me like family, let me come over whenever I want, and even jump in the whip. Lol nigga I love you fam. And to all the people out there who have technical needs, Tv Mounting, Audio and Video, Security Cameras, Commercial and Residential, Computer Repair and builds, Cabling, Networking, and Phone Lines. Holla at my boy: T. POPE TECHNICAL SOLUTIONS. tpope2022@yahoo.com.

To my cousin Johnny: Thanks for everything you've done when I needed you.

To my sister's: Cirstie, Kelia, Danyette, Markena, and Rre...I love y'all.

To my nephews: Bj, Zanthius, John Jr, Johnathan, TJ and Devon...I love y'all.

To my nieces: Kamill and Anyce, I love y'all.

To my daughters: Payden, I love you and it's not a day that pass, I don't think about you. I look forward to spending time with you when I touch down...

Kailynn: I miss you too! Even though you actin' funny with a nigga. Lol I love you and can't wait to spend time with you.

To my nigga Solizzal: Yeah nigga you thought I wasn't gone put you down but real niggas keep it real at all time. I love you fam. To all the music fans out there, check out my boy from Waco Texas! The nigga live real talk.soundcloud.com/solizzal.

To my baby momma: Yeah, it's real! I want you to know that I really appreciate you for bringing my daughter into this world and giving me another reason to go hard. Regardless of how much we fight, I want you to know that I'm proud of you and your accomplishments. I know that it's a lot of mother's out there who's not making sure that their kids are safe. But you're a wonderful mother. True Story!

To my nigga Justin: I appreciate you fam, you been my nigga since the 5th grade and I want you to know that I love you. Yeah we may fight with each other from time to time. But we know what it is: You need to take yo' crazy medicine! LMFAO.

To my nigga Patrick: Say nigga I love you fam, you always been 1,000 with me and you ain't never forgot about me since I been gone. I can't wait to touch down and get in the booth with you.

To Crystal: Now I gotta say, you are one of the realest females alive! Out of every woman I have come in contact with, you fucked with me the hardest. When I had nobody it was you I could lean on. You done more for me than everybody who scream they love me. Except for my mom and dad! Real talk, you showed me the definition of a real friend. You stood by me and helped me build this shit and not once did you ask me for a dime. Even when I offered you shit you always turned it down. SMH...But I understand that you just wanted to see me live my dream, and you showed me that by helping me get to where I am right now. I really appreciate you for that and I want you to know that I love you from the bottom of my heart.

To all my niggas on lock: Sebastian Sion, Deunjerelle Jackson, Jevorish Ford, Fresh, Roderick Corpenter, Katrel Childs, Davion Griffin, Larry Adams, Raephil Johnson, Jonas Rambo, Curtis Criss, Gary Riwens, Larry Carson, Thash Thompson, Donald Bernard, Be Morris, Richard Mathis, Roman Rarnes, Dude, Yella, Rodney, and Lil Jay. I love you niggas, y'all always been 1,000 with me so it's only right I acknowledge the real.

To all my fans: I want to thank ya'll. Be on the look out for the authors I'm about to introduce. I promise K@SH HOUSE about to set fire to your imagination!

C@SINO DI@MOND$

CHAPTER 1

$$$

May, 2006

"Trap Money Cartel!" everybody screamed.

It was the 20th anniversary of the Trap Money Cartel. The crowd rolled to Club Nite Moves to party with the Trap Money Cartel. The club was packed, and the DJ had everyone turned up and vibing as he spun record after record. Some women were shaking their ass on the dancefloor like they were trying to make the cut on an Uncle Luke video. Men were at the photobooth with their crew taking pictures with random chicks holding stacks and knots, acting like they are balling holding two-hundred ones sandwiched between two franklins. The bar was packed with want-to-be macks shooting game at the females while the hoodrats roached up on free drinks. The real ballers were buying out the bar and sitting in VIP with the baddest bitches in the city smoking loud, popping X, and playing with their nose. While the high maintenance bitches sat in VIP with their noses up, roaching up a good time.

Trap Money was the boss of the northside of Houston. He always gave out school supplies, backpacks, footlocker gift cards, and uniforms for the kids going back to school. He paid teens to cut the older folks' yards and wash their cars. He even made sure that they had store runners if they needed them. The hood was always taken care of. This made a lot of people love and respect him, and tonight they showed how much they cared.

"Daddy, it's off the chain in here!" Trap Money's daughter, Rowdy, shouted.

"Yeah, I know. Look at yo sister over there, shakin' her ass like I ain't in here."

Rowdy laughed then ran on the dance floor to help her sister break the other girls off.

Trap Money had three kids, but the twins were his heart. Most people looked at them and thought them to be squares because they were so beautiful. But the girls were far from that title. Trap Money had groomed all three of his kids to be bosses.

The girls were identical twins, standing five foot three and weighing 130 pounds with asses like a question mark. They were light-skinned with hazel eyes and long wavy hair. Lil Moma was the quiet type, but Rowdy was loud and crazy about everything.

Trap Money had the girls trained to be killas. He didn't want anyone to ever think that his girls were his weakness. So a lot of people found out the hard way that Lil Moma and Rowdy ain't to be fucked with.

He had also groomed his son, teaching him everything there was to know about the game, and Dawg Face became ruthless like his dad.

"Smoke Dawg in this bitch!" said Smoke Dawg as he walked into the VIP area. Smoke Dawg was Trap Money's baby brother. People thought he was just a pretty boy, mostly 'cause he favored the actor Terrence Howard. But just like his brother, he too was merciless.

2

Smoke Dawg was 5'11, 225 pounds and had a head full of hair. Females always wanted to braid his hair, mostly for braggin' rights. So Smoke Dawg always had some fly braids.

Their father, on the other hand, was a brown-skinned, bald headed nigga.. He stood 6'3 with 285 pounds of muscle. Trap used to play basketball and was about to go to the NBA before tearing his ACL and being dismissed by the league. After five years of working different 9-to-5s, he started selling weed until he met this Haitian in Miami named Diamond Dawg. Diamond Dawg taught Trap Money everything he could, and Trap Money became very wealthy and powerful. Diamond Dawg had been more than the plug; he became Trap Money's friend. Whenever Trap Money needed advice, he would get on the plane and fly to Miami.

"Trap Money, man, we got this bitch packed!" Smoke Dawg told his brother.

"Yeah, just wait until Z-Ro and Slim Thug hit the stage," Trap Money responded.

And just when the people thought the club was already crunk, Z-Ro came through.

"Oh, my God! Oh, my God!" the groupies screamed as they tried to take pictures of the star. "Look, Z-Ro in here!"

Z-Ro jumped on the stage and rocked the crowd. And just when they thought he was finished, Slim Thug came in and joined him to hit a few of their songs together. The party couldn't get any better.

Trap Money was blowin' some dro and enjoying his moment. Twenty years in the game, he now felt he needed to pull up and give his kids their moment to shine. He planned on giving his son the crown, but he had to make sure he was hungry for it. Not everyone was fit to be king. This was something he learned over the years of hustlin'.

About two hours later, Trap Money decided it was time to leave. He told everybody he was about to head home and went to holla at Dawg Face. When he made it to where Dawg Face was, he could do nothing but laugh. Dawg Face was on the floor dancing with the twins' friend, Checkmate.

Checkmate was a dark-skinned girl who favored the tennis player, Sloan Stephens. She was 5'4, 140 pounds, and also had long, wavy hair. Most men took her looks for weakness, but Checkmate was heartless. She was the type of woman who remained loyal to you if she loved you, but if you crossed her, she would kill. The twins were her closest friends, the only ones who truly understood her. She had been through so much at a young age, and the twins were the only people who knew her story.

Checkmate and Dawg Face were cool, but because they were so much alike, they were always fighting.

Trap Money watched his son do his thang on the dance floor. After another ten minutes, he told his son that he was leaving and he wanted to ride with him so they could talk.

Dawg Face told Checkmate he was leaving then kissed his sisters and told them goodbye.

Once they left the club, Dawg Face jumped in the front passenger seat of his father's S550. Trap Money hit Hwy 1960 and took the long way home. He and his kids had separate houses in Kingwood. He had purchased a hundred acres of land and had four houses built on it. He wanted his children to have their own spots, and he made sure everybody was safe because their land was gated with cameras all around the property.

"Dawg Face, it's time for you to take over the game," Trap Money said. "I had my run and now it's our turn. Do you want this lifestyle or what?"

"Yeah, Pops," Dawg Face responded. "I can handle it. I'm ready." His excitement was evident.

"Dawg Face, you got to understand. This game will breed envy. Niggas will hate the way you are about to take my spot. People will hate how you are so young in this position, and some won't respect you in the beginning. They will feel you didn't earn shit; they will feel that I just gave this shit to you.

"But that's something I'm not doing. You will build yo own cartel. All I will do is supply you with the connects. Son, in order for you to be respected and feared, y'all have to be ruthless. You want a motherfucka to believe y'all don't give a fuck about life itself. Money and murder equal power. Feed yo cartel 'cause you never want yo team to be jealous of you in no way.

"Never allow yo'self to be accessed. Do you see how we live? I protected my family by surroundin' y'all with killas. Are we untouchable? No. But we damn sure not easy targets.

"I will give you all the information you need to have. You need to make a trip to Miami to meet your connect. His name is Diamond Dawg. Now, I'm warning you. That's a ruthless motherfucka. If you cross him, I can't save you. He way stronger than my team, so make sure yo bizness straight. And if you meet his granddaughters, I advise you not to try to fuck with 'em. And I'm talking about in a sexual way. Never mix bizness with pleasure or you won't last."

He hoped his son listened.

In his mind, though, Dawg Face had already taken over. When he got to his house, he sat and thought about everything his dad told him. After an hour of brainstorming, he finally had everything planned out. The next morning, he would put it in motion.

*****

Dawg Face woke up the next morning and checked his phone. He read his text messages and saw that his sisters had made it home safe. He then called his boys Damn Fool and Square Bizness. Once they told him that they were on the way, he got Rowdy on the phone.

"Boy, why the hell you callin' me so damn early?!" Rowdy asked.

"Girl, get up. I need to run some plays by y'all, so be here in an hour."

"Yeah, alright, but this shit better be important," Rowdy told him and hung up. She had already figured out that it was important because he never called that early. After she got up and took a bath, she got dressed. Her, Lil Moma, and Checkmate went to Dawg Face's house.

Damn Fool and Square Bizness also made it to the house and Dawg Face began his meeting.

Dawg Face sat in his chair looking like a younger version of Trap Money. He stood five foot nine, 185 pounds. His skin was brown just like his dad's, but he had long braids. His boy, Damn Fool sat next to him. That man was just that: a damn fool. He was always smiling and playing, but quick to bust yo head. Damn Fool was six foot one and weighed 165 pounds. He wore his hair in a bald fade, was always fly, and kept a bad female.

Now Square Bizness was what you called the enforcer. He was a man that people got nervous around. Square Bizness towered at 6'4 and was a hefty 315 pounds. He was supposed to play in the NFL on the line but decided the streets were his home. He was a junior in college when he got caught with some drugs and guns. That messed up his chances of going pro. Most people didn't understand him, not even Dawg Face, but he would never judge him about his issues.

"Look, I called y'all five to my spot because I wanted to let y'all know I just got the keys to the city. I'm startin' my own empire called

Black Diamond Cartel. Trap Money gave me his blessings and all of his connects. He decided that he is about to retire.

"I want y'all to be my underbosses. Each one of you will have and be in charge of your own crew. I will only deal with y'all. If someone in your crew fuckin' up, I hold y'all responsible because you brought them into our family. If anybody don't want in, then excuse yourself now and it's no love lost."

After no one got up, he went on with his speech. "Now Trap Money got the city on lock. But I want more than Houston. I want Texas. In order for us to make that happen, we got to build a strong team of killas like us. Also, we have to wipe out Trap Money Cartel 'cause once Trap Money retires, then it's over for them. We wanna be able to eat without them in our way."

He looked at each of them to see where they were at.

"So you think Trap Money gonna just let us kill his team and not do shit?" Rowdy asked.

"He's retiring so that shit no longer should matter. But if it do, then he's just gonna have to be fucked up about it, 'cause his team in our way."

Damn Fool asked, "Do you think they gonna stay loyal once it's understood he's out the game and they gotta get dope from his 20-year-old son?"

Everyone had to admit he made a lot of sense, but Dawg Face didn't answer.

"So what's the meaning behind you namin' the squad Black Diamond Cartel?" Checkmate asked.

"Because the black diamond is the toughest form of natural, industrial diamond. It is an impure form of polycrystalline diamond, graphite, and amorphous carbon. Its natural color is black or dark grey, and it is more porous than other diamonds."

All of them were not only impressed by his explanation, but also by the fact that he considered them Black Diamonds.

"So from now on," he continued, "call me Karbonado, which is known as the Black Diamond."

They all nodded their heads and the meeting ended.

It was time to put together a deadly team.

*****

Trap Money

Trap Money was on his way to his old stomping grounds, Kashmere Garden, was where he was born and raised. He always made it his business to stop through, checking on his workers from time to time. He also was riding around thinking about the fallout had with Young Hogg.

Young Hogg wanted him to drop the price on the bricks he was buying, but Trap Money refused. Trap Money told him ten thousand a brick was love, and that was cheap for it to be uncut.

Trap Money dialed Young Hogg.

"Yo, what's up?" Young Hogg answered.

"Say, man, I thought about what you said, and I decided, fuck it. If you don't want to spend the ten, then I'll just cut you all the way out! I fed yo whole team and you act like a nigga owe you somethin'."

"Nigga, fuck you! You act like a nigga need you! Matta fact, suck my dick. That's what you can do." The anger roiled from Young Hogg.

"Nigga, you a dead man walkin'. It's on site!"

There was no way Young Hogg was about to live. As he was riding down Hirsch, he got a call from Rowdy. "Hey, baby girl, what's up?" he asked.

"Why you sound like that?" Rowdy could tell something was wrong with her daddy.

Trap Money told her what happened then asked her if Karbonado gave her his plans.

She told him what she thought of them.

After ten minutes of talking to her, he got a call from Smoke. "Baby girl, let me call you back. This uncle Smoke Dawg."

Trap Money ended his call then clicked over. "What's up, nigga?"

"Man, I need you to swing by so we can rap about some plays," Smoke Dawg told his brother.

"A'ight. I'll swing by in about thirty minutes."

*****

"Good. Now all you got to do is get him to talk about drugs and discuss his plug." The detectives next to Smoke coached him on what to say.

Smoke Dawg had been pulled over coming out of Gulf Coast Apartments. When the cops searched his car after smelling weed, they found two handguns, two pickle jars full of molly, and thirty thousand cash in the trunk. He was a convicted felon already, so he was facing life. The feds gave him a chance to save himself by giving up his connect, and his brother was all he knew.

He waited on his brother but Trap Money never came by, and that didn't sit right with Smoke Dawg. Smoke called Trap Money multiple times but never got a response. He explained to the detectives that he didn't know what was up.

*****

Trap Money was about to head to Smoke Dawg's spot, but he got a call from a detective asking him about a murder that took place at Nite Move the night of his party. Trap Money was so busy arguing and cursing the detectives out, he didn't notice the red truck pull up on the side of him. A man was hanging out the back window with an AK47.

BRRTTT, BRRTTT.

Trap Money tried to pull off, but he was ambushed by the powerful rifle.

Someone had just made the mistake of murdering the boss of all bosses.

There was no way that the Trap Money Cartel would not retaliate.

*****

Lil Moma was watching *The Jamie Foxx Show* when it was interrupted with breaking news. She couldn't believe what she was seeing. She jumped up and called Rowdy who picked up on the third ring. "What's up, Moma?" she answered, sounding like she was hollering as usual.

"Rowdy, have you seen the news? Trap Money got killed!"

"What?" Rowdy asked in shock. "Have you talked to Karbonado?"

"No, but we need to get him on the phone. Hold up and let me three-way him."

He couldn't believe that someone murdered their pops. They planned to paint the city red.

Rowdy told him what Trap Money had said about Young Hogg.

Karbonado was about to eliminate Young Hogg and the Garden City Cartel.

CHAPTER 2

$$$

Two weeks later

It was a sad day. Everybody came to show their love and respect for Trap Money. The twins really took the death of their father hard. Even Checkmate was crying. She looked at Trap Money as a father figure. He had taught her a lot of things and for that she planned on getting revenge the day after he was buried.

Smoke Dawg and the members of the Trap Money Cartel all sat at the front. As the pastor gave his sermon, six men walked in. Everybody was now focused on them. Once they made it to the front of the church, they gave Smoke Dawg a hug. Everyone relaxed, seeing that the men were showing respect for Trap Money.

When Smoke Dawg's tension eased, one of the men pulled out a .357 and shot Smoke Dawg in the face.

Everybody in the church started screaming and trying to get out of the way. But the other five members had TEC-9 and were killing everything that was a part of the Trap Money Cartel.

11

TTTT, BRRRT, BRRRT!

Checkmate, Karbonado, and the twins had no guns. No one expected this to happen, and that was something that Karbonado and the rest of them would regret.

After killing the Trap Money Cartel, one of the members said something that nobody ever thought they would hear. "This city belong to the Garden City Cartel now!"

They walked out like nothing happened.

Blood was everywhere. Karbonado and the rest could not believe what happened. But one thing was for sure: The Garden City Cartel had fucked up by leaving him alive.

They had no clue about the Black Diamond Cartel.

And that's what he would use to his advantage.

*****

It had been non-stop killing. The Black Diamond Cartel had been going through all of Young Hogg's spots, killing with no remorse. Karbonado and his crew went to the Garden City projects where Young Hogg moved 60% of his drugs. The Black Diamond Cartel pulled up four trucks deep and Karbonado got out to approach them.

"What's up, fam?" Big Ken asked.

Karbonado pulled his gun out and hit him across the nose.

"Aggghh!" Big Ken cried out.

Shut the fuck up!" Karbonado told him. He reached in his pocket, pulled out a phone, and told Big Ken to call Young Hogg.

Big Ken did as he was instructed.

"Yo, what up?" Young Hogg answered.

"You fucked up not killin' me. Now I'ma kill you and everything a part of you."

BOOM! BOOM!

Karbonado shot Big Ken in the head then dropped the phone.

As he was walking to the truck, the rest of his team started shooting.

It was an all-out war between the Garden City Cartel and the Black Diamond Cartel. Karbonado was forced to leave because they were outnumbered, but he planned to return later and finish what he started.

*****

"Ain't this a bitch! First, somebody killed Trap Money then they killed Smoke Dawg. And to make matters worse, nobody knows shit!" Detective Carter was mad as hell. His partner, Detective Moore, just listened as she was trying to formulate a plan. But it was hard when no one was talking.

The two detectives were going to work on these cases day and night until they figured out what was what. They knew that if they solved any of these cases, they could end up getting a promotion.

As they were talking and reviewing paperwork, they got a call about murders that took place in the Garden City Projects.

Finally, maybe they had a break.

The two detectives grabbed their keys, guns, and jackets and they rushed out the door. Once Detective Carter and Detective Moore made it to the projects, they could not believe what they were seeing. After they took in the scene, the detectives decided to walk around and question a few people to see if they could gather any information.

An hour later, they still hadn't come up with anything. The detectives were so pissed they wanted to plant something on somebody just to get them to talk. But just when they were about to give up, a young girl named Mariah gave the detectives a lead.

"All I heard was the guy say something about it's game over, then he shot Big Ken two times in the face. After that, he dropped Big Ken's phone and walked off. Then some more people with him started shootin'."

The detectives couldn't believe how bold the shooters were. Detective Carter asked the young girl for her name, then asked how old she was.

After she told them her name and that she was sixteen, Detective Carter cursed because their luck had run out.

"Got dammit!"

Detective Moore pulled him to the side and stated, "We can't use her. She a minor. We not even supposed to talk to her without her parents' permission."

Detective Carter knew she was right, but he had an idea. He walked back to the young girl and asked, "Didn't you say he dropped Big Ken's phone after shootin' him?"

"Yes," she answered.

The two detectives smiled and told the girl thanks. They walked off, rushing to where Big Ken's body laid ten minutes earlier. After talking to a couple of investigators, they took possession of Big Ken's' phone. They got in their car and headed to the station to see if they could get any fingerprints other than Big Ken's off his phone.

CHAPTER 3

$$$

A week later, Karbonado was walking through the Gucci store in the Galleria Mall. He and Rowdy were always together, tearing up the stores. As he was getting ready to pay for their selections, he noticed a beautiful woman walk in the store. She stood 5'4, 130 pounds, and she was *bad*. Her hair was short with a nice taper around her sides and back the top was flipped up and curled back real clean cut look with a red under tone to make the color on her hair pop out. She favored the singer, Janelle Monae.

Rowdy noticed that her brother was focused on someone, and when she looked around, she was speechless. Her brother left her at the counter and went to meet Janelle Monae.

Karbonado walked over to her and gave his opinion on the shoes she was trying on. "Me and those shoes were made just for you," he said.

Janelle Monae looked up at a smiling Karbonado. She knew he had money; he was dressed in money from head to toe. From the diamonds in his watch, chain, ring, ears, and mouth, she knew he was either a drug dealer or a rapper.

"What makes you believe that?" she asked.

"Because the Bible say it's not good for a man to be alone," he replied.

"You right," she said smiling. "But you said man. Just 'cause you alone don't mean that I am alone."

Karbonado grabbed her hand and kissed it. "Because you ain't got a ring on yo finger, that tell me you ain't got a husband or you ashamed to tell people you married to his ass." He had her cheesin' from ear to ear. "Look, I been losin' for the last few years. Stop playin' and let a nigga win." He wouldn't let up.

Rowdy then told her, "Girl, you gon' give this nigga yo number or you gone stand here all day? 'Cause he ain't gone give up."

She just couldn't stop laughing. Her best friend Kiara was even laughing with her. She had to admit, Karbonado had a slick mouth piece.

She reached for her purse and handed him a business card. "Kaci Conner, Attorney at Law," Karbonado read out loud.

"Since you know my name, what's yours?" she asked.

"Well, it depends," he responded.

"On what?"

"Shit, on the timing. Some call me Jason, some call me Karbonado. But women tend to call me Papi."

She laughed again then started to end their conversation.

"Well, look. I don't want to hold my friend up. We have something to take care of, so hit me up when you get the time, Mr. Jason."

He agreed to call her later that night.

Once they ended their conversation, Rowdy let him have it. "Nigga, you think you so fly!" she told him.

"Whatever, Rowdy. I'm that nigga every woman dream about. The only reason you ain't dreamin' about me, shit, you can't think. You so dumb you don't even know how to dream!"

Rowdy couldn't do nothing but laugh. "Fuck you!" she responded.

*****

Kaci and Kiara watched the two of them leave the store laughing.

"Girl, I know that nigga a drug dealer," Kiara told Kaci.

"How you know? Did he tell you that?"

"I am a cop. I know a drug dealer when I see one!"

"And that's the reason yo ass ain't got a man to jump in them guts at night," Kaci said laughing.

"Bitch, please. When the last time you had a man? We in the same dickless boat. The last time you had somebody touch that thang was when you were givin' birth to Asia, and we both know that pain wasn't pleasure."

Now it was Kiara laughing again.

Kaci had to admit she hadn't been touched by nobody in the past two years. She was so busy focused on her career and raising her two-year-old daughter Asia.

Kiara was beautiful with a caramel complexion. At 5'6, she carried her thick 145 pounds well. Her shoulder-length hair was silky smooth. Kiara was a very fine woman, but her job as a cop seemed to scare off a lot of men. Kaci always joked about the fact that she was a cop that couldn't make the proper arrest.

"Girl, how you a cop and can't handcuff one man? If I was a cop, I'd at least handcuff a nigga and take some dick," Kaci joked.

Every time men saw Kiara in uniform, they looked but went the opposite direction. Yet, men always seemed to approach her when she was in regular clothes. Once she seemed to find somebody cool to converse with, they stopped messing with her after she revealed that she was a cop. That made her dislike her job in a way.

Kiara decided to not waste her time meeting men. It had been at least a year since she had someone, but she was cool with the little friend in her dresser. She even nicknamed it the Munk Beater.

After Kiara and Kaci finished shopping, they went to eat at the Cheesecake Factory.

*****

Later that night, Karbonado was sitting at the house blowing dro and watching Kat Williams' stand-up comedy. After laughing at Kat, he paused the DVR and decided to call Kaci. She answered on the fourth ring.

"What's up, sexy?" Karbonado put on his smooth voice.

"Who is this?"

"Yo' rib," he replied.

"My what?" she asked, laughing.

"It's yo' rib callin'," Karbonado repeated.

"Umm, I just got out of the tub, and I know for a fact that every one of my ribs is right here with me," she said, a smile in her voice.

"Damn, you must not have been wearin' yo' glasses."

"Boy, you silly. What you up to?"

"Nothin'. I just wanted to hit you up, 'cause I'm a man of my word."

"Oh, I'll give you that, and I appreciate honesty. I'm also a woman of my word."

Kaci and Karbonado talked on the phone for hours. They damn near talked about everything. She told him how she was raising her daughter by herself. She was all the way open with him. She couldn't wait to hang out with him, though she wanted to ask him if he was a drug dealer but didn't know how.

"Can I ask you something before we hang up?" she asked.

"Yeah, what's up?"

"What is it that you do for a living?"

"Do it really matter?" Karbonado inquired.

"Well, yes, 'cause I feel if we gonna kick it, we should know who we kickin' it with. So what is it that you do? Where do you work?"

"Kaci, I'm self-employed. I get paid to live."

It was obvious that he wasn't going to say more, and all she could do was give a nervous chuckle. She didn't want to keep pushing it, so she left it alone for the time being.

By the time they got off the phone, it was 2:15 in the morning. Kaci never really stayed up late unless it was work-related. She was surprised she was having such a good time when she knew she was only going to get about four hours of sleep. She had to be up at 6AM and at the court house by eight to represent some clients.

She and Karbonado had made plans to go out on Friday, and she was excited about seeing him.

*****

The next day, Karbonado was still in his bed sleeping when his front door came crashing in.

Karbonado heard the loud noise, but before he could make it all the way out of the bed, he had four officers pointing guns in his face.

"Put your hands up! Get on the ground, now!"

Karbonado did as he was told and one of the cops placed their cuffs on him and took him to the front room. He convinced one of the officers to allow him to get his lawyer's number out of his phone.

19

"Her name is Kaci Conner," he told the cop.

After the officer gave him the number, he memorized it and sat quietly while they did what they had come to do. The cops were tearing his house up. They found a few guns, but the one they were looking for wasn't there. They knew the murder weapon was a .357, but after an hour of searching the house, they had come up empty handed.

They transported Karbonado to the Harris County jail. While he was in the car, all he could think of was how they got in the gate. He knew that his sisters didn't let them in 'cause they were at Checkmate's house. Plus, there was no way they would let them in without calling to warn him. Just when he began to accept that they had broken the gate, it hit him that he forgot to hit the button to close it when he got home.

"Damn, I fucked up," he said to himself.

Once he made it to the Harris County jail, they began processing him. He knew he wouldn't be able to reach Kaci. She had already told him she would be busy until 5:00 that evening and would call him around 6:30. After several hours of waiting to make it to the floor, he was finally taken to the seventh floor. Because his case was capital murder, they placed him in a single man cell on 23-hour lockdown.

He had already called and told Rowdy what was going on. She had ordered everyone to chill until Karbonado got out because she didn't want anything to affect his case.

Just as he settled in, a jailer called him on the intercom in his cell. "Lewis, you have a visit! Lewis, you have a visit!"

Karbonado went to visitation area. He wasn't expecting nobody, so he was surprised when they walked him to an attorney booth.

After they locked him in the glass booth, he smiled and asked, "How you know I was in here?"

"Because you were on the news," Kaci said with disappointment.

"Well, look, can you represent me or is this out of your league?" He got straight to the point.

"Yeah, I can represent you, but can you afford me?" She had to ask because no matter how much she had been feeling him, he wouldn't have her working for nothing.

"Hell yeah, I can afford it. Just tell me the cost." Being arrested hadn't caused him to lose some of that arrogance.

She paused for a second. She didn't want to charge him the kind of money the case was worth, but this was business and she had a child to take care of. "I charge $15,000 for a murder. You are being charged with fifteen murders. That's $225,000. Can you pay that?"

Karbonado put his head down, then he looked at her and shook his head.

Kaci grabbed her things and got up to leave.

"Damn, where you goin'?" he asked.

"Look, this is business, and you can't take care of it so let's not waste each other's time."

"I don't understand you lawyers, mainly the ones from the slums. You tryna charge me top dollar like you the best attorney in the state! Ain't nobody ever heard of yo' low budget ass. You know damn well you ain't never seen that type of money in yo' life. But I respect the fact that you ain't settlin' for less. Get ya money, baby. Call my sister. She will give you the money. But damn, for that type of money, can I get a bond?"

Kaci couldn't believe he had the $225,000 nor that he was willing to spend it with her. He was right; she was a no-name attorney and had never seen anything close to that kind of money. Plus, she hated that he was willing to pay her that much money and she wouldn't be able to get him a bond. There was no way he was getting out while facing fifteen murder charges.

"Jason, I will never get you a bond with all those murders pending. They will definitely consider you a flight risk."

He understood all of this and told her so to make her feel better.

She promised she would put her all into his case, and she meant it. She asked him about the murders he had been charged with, and he denied every one of them.

In a way she believed him, but something told her she wasn't getting the whole story.

CHAPTER 4

$$$

Kaci had been working day and night on Karbonado's case for three months. She'd discovered that his prints were found at the murder scene. That was a bad look on his part. She grabbed her keys and went to visit him.

"What's up, Ms. Connor?" he said, happy to get out of the cell.

She got straight to the point. "They can place you on the scene, so what is it you are not telling me?"

"What do you mean, they can place me at the scene?" he asked.

"Nigga, stop the fuckin' bullshit! They found your prints on the victim's phone. So you tellin' me you wasn't there? In order for me to fight for you, I gotta know what I'm dealing with. Now be real with me 'cause I'm tryna help yo' ass!" Her voice grew louder with each word.

"Okay. I popped the nigga's top! The motherfuckas murdered my dad!" He got loud too. "But do they have a witness?"

Kaci couldn't believe she was dealing with a killer.

Karbonado explained how he had only shot that one person and that he had gotten rid of the weapon.

She sat across from him appalled, yet intrigued as a million thoughts assaulted her, mentally and emotionally. In her mind she knew that she couldn't represent him by law. But at the same time in her heart she knew that she would have done the same thing had it been her mother. Just the thought of him going to these extremes behind those he loves eased her early apprehensions. This gave Kaci something to work with, and also something to look forward to. She would be ready when they went to trial the following week.

Kaci had been in the news a lot over the last three months because the case had been high profile. She wanted to win this case bad. If she won, then she would most likely get other serious cases and her stock would go up.

*****

It was crazy in the courtroom. Nobody thought that this no -name lawyer would beat all of the murder cases Karbonado had been facing. She put up a good fight and argued the facts well. The district attorney had to admit that he was impressed with her work. And due to Kaci beating all those charges, Karbonado was now being called Mr. Untouchable.

The day couldn't get any better. Kaci felt like she was on top of the world. She made some good money, got a lot of publicity, and won all on the same day.

"So what you gonna do tonight?" Karbonado asked.

"I'm going to go home and have me a drink, then call it a night," she responded.

24

"Damn, can't we get together and celebrate?" he asked with a smile on his face.

"Nigga, just 'cause you paid me a lot of money don't give me a reason to open my legs!" she told him.

"Damn. Hold up, Kaci. I ain't even said shit about yo' legs or anything like that."

"My bad. You right. But just look at it from my view. You just paid a broke bitch a quarter mill then you spent three months without any sex, and the first thing you say is that you want to celebrate. I know how you big money people think."

"I ain't even on that. I'm a boss and I can get sex any time I want it. I just wanted to celebrate with you. But it's cool. I'll just take a raincheck."

She laughed then walked off.

*****

That evening, Karbonado was at the house chillin' and talking with his sisters and Checkmate. They ate homemade fried chicken while talking shit. Checkmate and Karbonado teamed up to play Spades against the twins. They had been winning before Checkmate ended up getting them set.

"I thought you said you had four books?" Karbonado asked.

"I did, but they started cuttin'," she explained.

"Checkmate, yo' dumb ass counted a queen!" he told her.

She hadn't realized it until he pointed it out, but she got mad 'cause he was clownin' her. "Nigga, fuck you!" she said and threw her cards at him.

This had Rowdy and Lil Moma rolling hard.

25

Checkmate got up and left out of the room. She was so angry she had to smoke a blunt.

Karbonado got up and followed her outside. "Damn, Mate, it's like that?" he asked.

"Nigga, you know how I hate when you talk to me like I'm stupid. I told you multiple times I hate that shit!"

"Damn, Checkmate. I was just playin' but you can't get mad 'cause yo' ass fucked up." He chuckled at her 'tude.

No matter how mad he or the twins got her, she could never stay mad. She had been around them for the past ten years.

"Checkmate, you know I need you to turn the fuck up. I know these Garden City Cartel niggas think I'm shook up from this murda trial. But that's where you come in at.

"I'm gone need to dip to Miami and holla at the plug. While I'm gone, I need to turn up the murda rate. I'll have an alibi 'cause I'll be in Miami. Do 'em and make a statement."

"I got you. Don't worry. Go take care of everything you need to take care of." She promised she would put in work.

That is what he loved the most about Checkmate. She was a loyal rider.

After talking, they went back in the house, and Rowdy had to start some shit. "Y'all got y'all game plan now? Or do y'all need some more time to talk?" Lil Moma burst out laughing.

"Fuck both of y'all," Karbonado and Checkmate said at the same time.

While they were laughing, Karbonado got a phone call. The caller said he was a friend of his dad's and wanted to meet up to reveal some important things to him. Karbonado agreed to meet with him the next morning. After talking to J-Money, Karbonado decided to call it a night. He told the girls to lock the door whenever they left.

26

*****

The next morning, Karbonado woke up and got ready to meet this J-Money cat. When he went to get something to drink, he noticed Checkmate was asleep on the couch. The kitchen had been cleaned, so he figured that she had stayed up late and scrubbed everything down.

He went to Checkmate and woke her up. "Damn, girl, you need to take yo' ass home."

"Man, you better leave me alone. I stayed up and cleaned that kitchen last night by myself."

"Well I'm 'bout to go meet up with this nigga. He got some info about my dad. You wanna ride with me?"

"Yeah. I'll roll, but you gotta give me thirty minutes to shower and get dressed." She always kept clothes at his and the girls' spot 'cause she was always with them.

After five minutes, they were heading out the door. Once they arrived at the address J-Money gave him, Karbonado gave Checkmate two 9s. She placed each gun on the inside of each of her thighs. Karbonado knew that these boys might want to search him, but would never think Checkmate had anything under her dress.

They got out of the car and went inside the warehouse where they were escorted to the back room. When they entered the back room, they both were surprised to see that it was Justin Fisher, the district attorney.

Karbonado was glad Checkmate was with him because he now felt like it was a setup.

"Have a seat, Mr. Lewis. Or should I call you Mr. Untouchable?"

Karbonado looked at him and smiled. "Just call me the man not to fuck with."

Justin Fisher smiled himself. Karbonado was always cocky.

"You wasn't so cocky when I had you by the balls."

"Yeah, you right. Until you was forced to let 'em go." Karbonado was feeling himself.

Ignoring Karbonado, the DA turned toward Checkmate. "Alexis Carter, how are you? Or should I call you Checkmate?"

"You don't know me, motherfucka. Don't call me shit. Matter fact, don't even talk to me." Checkmate was being very aggressive.

"Look, I didn't call y'all here to see whose heart is bigger. If it wasn't for your dad, I would have fried yo' ass in court."

"What the fuck you mean, if it wasn't for my pops?" Karbonado asked .

"Listen. Yo daddy is my cousin. My mother and your granny were sisters." He paused for a second before continuing. "Nobody knows that we are related, and it must stay that way. I will give you the same protection I gave your dad in court."

Justin Fisher pulled out his iPhone and pushed play. He handed Karbonado the phone.

Checkmate and Karbonado couldn't believe what they were watching. He had just witnessed himself murder Big Ken then have a shoot-out in Garden City.

"How the fuck you get this?" he asked.

"Technology. There's a light pole in Garden City as soon as you come in. The camera sits at the top. Yo' pops had them put up to monitor Garden City. Now do you believe me?"

Karbonado knew that he wasn't playin'. If he wanted to fry him, he was fried. Justin Fisher had promised to protect his team in the courts, and he couldn't refuse that type of power.

"But I need you to do one thing," he told Karbonado.

"What's that?"

"Send Ms. Kaci Conner to me. She is now famous because of us. So we need to keep her on our team. You can trust her. Most lawyers get cases and they trade people's freedom for money. We offered her thirty grand to sell you out and she refused. Had she sold you out, she would have died before trial. She didn't, so we need to keep her on the team."

Karbonado loved what he was hearing. Even Checkmate felt the power they had just gained.

Justin Fisher, aka J-Money, was about to put money in Kaci's pocket and help Karbonado take over the city.

*****

Kaci was at home relaxing in the tub and listening to Sade's "By Your Side." She felt good about winning the case that most people considered impossible. As she soaked, she got a call from the district attorney, Justin Fisher, asking to meet for lunch the next day.

At first, she wasn't up for it, but he explained that he wanted to discuss something very important. She finally agreed and they ended the call.

Kaci's mind raced, wanting to know what he was up to, but she would have to wait until the next day to find out.

Her day had now moved on; she was already on tomorrow.

CHAPTER 5

$$$

Kaci arrived at Chili's to meet with Justin Fisher. He was already there waiting on her. She took a seat and looked at the menu to see what she wanted.

Once they ordered their food, Justin Fisher started explaining the reason for the meeting. "Look, Ms. Connor, I know you're wondering what this meeting is about." She nodded and he continued. "Well, I must admit that you put up a damn good fight in court. You could have easily given up, but you showed you wasn't a quitter. I would love for us to team up. You could really become the best attorney in the U.S."

Kaci didn't understand, so she asked him what he meant.

"What I'm about to tell you can't leave this table." He pulled out his iPhone and showed her the same video he had shown Karbonado. When she finished watching, he continued. "There was no way you could have beat me in court had I revealed this piece of evidence. But because I'm on Karbonado's team, I let you win.

"And because of that, you have been all over the news as one of the best up and coming attorneys. So I'm here to make you an offer. As long as you represent Karbonado and his team, you will win every case and become a millionaire. I will guarantee you cases will go your way every single time. I am plugged in with judges, cops, and the mayor. I can weaken any case against you so that you will win at trial or even have it thrown out before a trial starts. All you gotta do is what you been doin'. Yo' job. What do you say?"

He waited as she sat stunned by all of this information and everything he had laid on the table. In the end, he had made her an offer she couldn't refuse.

"We have a deal," she responded.

"Kaci, just take my advice. You are now a high profile lawyer. You should only accept cases worthy of your talent, and you should charge $30,000 just to take a case while never making less than a hundred grand to go to trial. Every case you win, I get $20,000. I'll have you wire it to an offshore account."

After he finished speaking, he stood and offered to shake on the deal. "Oh, yeah. This will be the last time we communicate in public." He gave her his card, and said, "Inform me when you get a case."

He left her with her thoughts as she remembered always growing up as a kid feeling helpless as her father was sent away for life and she couldn't believe Karbonado put her in a position to become a powerful and wealthy attorney.

*****

Karbonado was getting ready to fly to Miami to meet the man they called the Diamond Dawg. While he was at the airport, he talked to

Rowdy, Lil Moma, and Checkmate. Each of them had a mission to accomplish.

Rowdy and her team were supposed to make a statement in Gulf Coast. Checkmate and her crew were looking to handle the Garden City Projects. And Lil Moma was to take her group and make a statement in Havastock.

Everything was planned for them to do it while he was in Miami, because once he got back, he would flood the city with dope.

The Black Diamond Cartel was about to be untouchable, and soon the hustlers would want to join the team.

Karbonado was about to take advantage of every opportunity he could get. He wanted to take over Texas. It was so much money.

With the help of Justin Fisher, he planned on getting every dime.

*****

This was the first time that Karbonado had been to Miami. He had been off the plane for five minutes and was already in love with the beautiful view. He had already started making plans mentally to bring his crew down to Miami and party.

Once he called Diamond Dawg, it didn't take but fifteen minutes for a Rolls Royce Phantom to pull up. Karbonado wasn't that impressed because his dad had one.

The driver got out of the car and grabbed Karbonado's bags and placed them in the trunk. He then opened the door to the back seat and allowed him to get in. Karbonado reclined his seat and enjoyed the view as he rode through Miami.

After approximately ten minutes, they pulled up to a house so big that Karbonado couldn't believe what he was seeing. "How many motherfuckas live in this bitch," he said to himself. He got out of the car and the driver walked him to the house.

Once inside, he could not believe how gorgeous the interior was. Crystal chandeliers bathed the room in a soft golden glow that reflected off of the Greek style white marble floor. A Renaissance painting of Davinchi, Michelangelo, and Sanzio Raffaello the two former of which Karbonado recognized, hung on the wall. He moved closer and read the plaque beneath the ladder and recognized the name Raphael. The room radiated with antiquity but what caught Karbonado eye was the antique golden gun collection there was a golden Musket, a Browning automatic rifle gilded in 24kt gold, an original 1911 Colt revolver cast in per rose gold, a tommy gun gold gilded from its era, beneath them all, on a tripod of pure gold sat a golden 19th century Gatling gun. Karbonado was awe struck as a large man with dreads came out of one of the rooms. The man looked at Karbonado then smiled.

"Karbonado, I'm glad to finally meet you." He walked up and shook his hand.

Karbonado was shocked to see that a Haitian was the plug. He expected to meet a Colombian or a Cuban, never a Haitian. His dad had a nice house but nothing like this.

"I'm glad to meet you too, Mr. Diamond Dawg," he responded.

"Make yourself at home. Whatever you need just let Boogie know and it will get taken care of. Don't be shy. Your dad was my boy, so we family.

"That's why I brought you to my house." Diamond Dawg's words really made Karbonado feel like family.

While they were talking, beautiful twin girls entered the house with a boatload of shopping bags. Karbonado was amazed by how pretty they were. The girls looked to be Latina and Black.

"Papa, it's been a long day," Twinkle said, excited to see Diamond Dawg.

Diamond Dawg beamed as he hugged the girls. "Twinkle, Star, this my friend Trap Money's son, Karbonado." He could tell that his guest liked the twins, but he said nothing. "Look, y'all are the same age, so I want you to take him around town and show him how we do it in MIA," Diamond Dawg told them.

They agreed and told Karbonado to jump fresh and be ready in an hour. The twins loved to party and they were about to show him how it was done.

"Those are my granddaughters. I nicknamed them Star and Twinkle. Me and your father always laughed about how we both had twins to spoil. That's something we had in common."

Karbonado could tell that this man really cherished his father's friendship. He was amazed at how cool Diamond Dawg was, but he remembered his father telling him that he was ruthless.

After talking for another twenty minutes, he went to jump in the shower and got ready to see the city with the girls.

*****

Back in Houston, it was sunny outside in Garden City: hustlers were hustlin', hoes were whorin', and kids were being kids. Checkmate came through with her team and changed the whole day. She got out of her car and walked up to one of the teens. She pulled out some money and asked one of the girls who was in charge.

"What do you mean 'in charge'?" the young girl asked.

"I mean who is the man that everybody listen to?"

"Oh. Well since you askin', then I know you not from around here, which mean you out of pocket. But since you got money in yo' hands, I'm gonna assume you gonna break me off." The girl held her hand out.

Checkmate laughed then peeled off ten, one hundred dollar bills. The young girl couldn't believe all the money she was now holding.

"Now tell me what I asked," Checkmate demanded.

"Tony Gunz stay in apartment nine," the girl told her.

"Good. Now listen to me carefully. Take yo' lil ass in the house and make sure you share that money with yo' friends. Don't ever change when you make a little change. Friends is priceless." The girl nodded, then Checkmate asked, "What's yo' name, and how old are you?"

"Jania, and I'm fifteen."

Checkmate didn't know what it was, but she took a liking to Jania. In a way, the girl reminded Checkmate of herself. "Do you have a cellphone?"

"No, my granny can barely afford food. So she damn sure can't get no cellphone." Jania looked Checkmate in the eyes, not ashamed of her lack of wealth.

"Well take some of that money and buy one."

Jania looked at the money, then back at Checkmate, and said, "I'm giving my three friends $100 a piece, then I wanted to help my granny pay a few bills. She's disabled so her check not much when you got bills and a granddaughter in high school."

Checkmate's eyes got a little shiny with tears. She had a teenager in front of her holding a rack, and she was willing to spend it all just to help her granny. "Come here," she told Jania.

She followed Checkmate to the car, and when they got there, Checkmate gave Jania the extra iPhone that she was gonna use for trapping. "Here, this yours. Don't worry about the bill. I'll keep it on, but you gotta promise me you will continue to go to school and take care of yo' granny."

"I promise," Jania said, unshed tears in her eyes.

Checkmate smiled and went in her purse and gave Jania five hundred dollars more. "To get you some fresh shoes, you and your three girls. Here's my number. Call me if you need anything, no matter what it is. And remember one thing: Don't ever lie to me."

"I promise I won't," Jania pledged.

"Good. Now take yo' friends and go in the house like I said and don't come out until after 3:30."

Jania said bye then got her friends and went into the house. She was so happy to have a little money and she planned to do what Checkmate told her to.

After Checkmate made sure Jania was in the house, she walked up to apartment nine. She knocked on the door and a female answered. Checkmate said, "Hey, I'm lookin' for Tony Gunz. Young Hogg sent me to deliver a message for him."

Hearing Young Hogg's name, the girl believed there was no threat. She opened the door and told Checkmate to come in. "He went to pick up some food. He should be back any minute now."

Checkmate went inside, and after she saw that it was just the girl and her daughter, she put her plan in motion. "Ah, she's so cute. Is this your baby?" She picked up the two year old. The baby was so pretty, Checkmate didn't want to put her down.

The girl, whose name was Monica, just smiled. "No, that's my niece. She Tony Gunz' daughter."

"Oh, so you Tony Gunz' sister?" Checkmate was feeling lucky.

"Yeah, Young Hogg and Tony Gunz are my big brothers."

Checkmate couldn't believe the shit that just fell in her lap. She had already left her crew outside behind tint. She heard the locks turn on the door and that's when Tony Gunz came through the door. He had some Timmy Chan's and was ready to eat. Once he put his food down, he noticed Checkmate.

She stood with the baby in one hand and a .357 in the other. It was pointed at the baby's head.

"Oh, my God!" Monica screamed, scared to death.

"Bitch, shut up befo' I start squeezin' on this bitch!" Checkmate said with her usual aggression.

Tony Gunz started talking. "Look, if it's money you want, I ain't got it here, but I can go down the street and get you whatever."

"Nigga, here's what I want. Call Young Hogg and hand me the phone. If you try anything stupid, I swear this baby head blown." Checkmate's warning was no joke.

Tony Gunz got Young Hogg on the phone and did as he was told.

"Say, bitch ass nigga," Checkmate said into the phone, "you think this beef over with? Well here's a message from the Black Diamond Cartel!"

BOOM! BOOM!

She shot Tony Gunz in the face then walked over to his body and pumped two more into his chest.

She was still holding the little girl who was now screaming at the top of her lungs.

Monica was still screaming as well. "Oh, my God! Please don't kill me! Please! I'm only nineteen."

Checkmate put the phone back to her ear. "You still think it's a game?" she asked Young Hogg.

He knew she wasn't playing. And because of the way his little sister was screaming, he knew Tony Gunz was dead. "Listen, let them make it 'cause this between us," he begged.

37

Checkmate started laughing. "When it's beef with us, it's only one rule we play by, and the rule is, everybody get it." She squeezed the trigger again, shooting Monica in the head. "Now, I got one more person left. Do you have an idea who could that be?" She asked the question with laughter ringing in her voice.

Young Hogg was now in tears and begging for her not to kill his two-year-old niece.

"You didn't give a fuck about Trap Money. Why should I give a fuck about this piece of shit niece of yours?"

"Look, I promise I'll let y'all be. Just let my niece live."

"I'll think about it," she said then hung up the phone.

She knew she wouldn't make it out of the projects alive so she would use the baby as a shield.

Checkmate placed the phone in her pocket so she could destroy it herself. She had learned from Karbonado's mistake. When she walked out of the house, she had the gun pointed at the baby's head again. Niggas was ready to kill her until they was forced to move back. They didn't want to deal with Young Hogg's niece being killed because of them.

The phone started ringing and she answered it. "Please, just don't kill my niece." Young Hogg begged again.

"Okay, I'll tell you what. Call yo' goons off and I'll let her live. But if they try me, I'm gonna kill her then be ready to die. Anyway it go, I will squeeze if you try me." He knew her threats were the real deal.

"Ask them for Block. Tell him I'm on the phone."

"Which one of you nigga's Block?" she asked.

"Me. What's up?" He was a kid who looked to be about sixteen.

"Come here. Young Hogg wanna holla."

Young Hogg told him to get in the truck, then she would drop him off at the corner store with the baby. He explained that he was to wait on him there and to tell everybody he said to fall back.

Block did what he was instructed to do and Checkmate made it out safe. She dropped Block off and told him to tell Hogg kids were off limits, but don't test her gangsta 'cause the next time a kid might die.

"And tell him I said enjoy the funerals."

CHAPTER 6

$$$

It was 8:00PM in Miami and Karbonado was hanging with the twins. He had only been around them for an hour and was really enjoying his time with them. He liked the fact that they just embraced him and treated him like family. They were so cool and he kept laughing about different shit. He loved how they walked around like they owned the city.

"Girl, look," Star said, pointing at some people. "She out of line comin' out the house with that ugly nigga!" They all started laughing. "Look at what he got on," she continued. "If you ugly, then you ugly. You can't do nothin' about that, but at least be fly. That way, if you try to holla at a bitch like me, I'll be like, 'This ugly ass nigga fly as hell.'"

"Star, leave them people alone," Twinkle told her.

But, of course, Star wouldn't leave it alone. "Hell no! Look at what he got on. Don't nobody sell FUBU no more, so how the hell he wearin' it? And look at his shoes. His ugly ass got on some Spreewells!" She had Karbonado and Twinkle rolling.

Star was one of those bad females that was quick to talk about you if you wasn't on point. She didn't give a damn. *Step yo swag up* was her motto.

She was a fly girl, a petite 5'2 and weighed a healthy 138 pounds with a nice sized ass. It wasn't like her sister's, but she damn sure had something to shake.

Now Twinkle was four inches taller and almost fifteen pounds heavier, and she had an ass like a reindeer. She also wore dreads that she kept neat.

After riding around and going to different spots, Karbonado and the twins decided to go home. The twins had enjoyed him and vice versa. They planned to show him more before he left the following day.

*****

Smoking some good Miami fire caused Karbonado to sleep like a baby, not to mention all of the yak he drank. His phone woke him up the next morning. When he looked at the screen, he saw it was Rowdy.

"Girl, why is you callin' me so damn early?!" he asked.

"Boy, I haven't heard from you and I just wanted to check on you," she replied.

"I'm good. I love it out here. I'll be back tomorrow though."

"Okay. Say, we put them plays down too. Checkmate went a lil overboard, though."

"What did she do?" he asked with very little concern.

"I'll tell you when you get home, but she did touch a nigga heart," she told him in code.

"Aight. I'ma holla at you when I get home."

"Yeah," she responded, "and Lil Moma say she love you, too!" Once he got off the phone, he got out of bed and went to get himself cleaned up. He was headed to the game room where he heard Diamond Dawg shooting pool.

"Did you have a good time last night?" Diamond Dawg asked.

"Yeah, I enjoyed myself. Them twins of yours had me laughin' and feelin' at home." He had a big grin on his face.

"You must be talking about Star. She's the one that keeps us all laughing." His look turned serious. "But let's talk business."

* * * * *

Several hours later, Karbonado and Diamond Dawg finished discussing business issues, and Karbonado couldn't wait to get the streets jumping. He knew that it wasn't nobody that could compete with his prices or the quality of his dope. He was supposed to kick it with the twins before he left, but he promised them that he would come back and party with them. He also invited them to Houston.

They were excited by the invite and agreed to go whenever he was ready. They had never been to H-Town, but they had heard it was a good city to party in.

* * * * *

After the stunt Checkmate pulled in Garden City, her name and the Black Diamond Cartel were buzzin' the streets. Niggas were now trying to get on the team. She planned on doing some more recruiting, but she wanted to make sure her first twenty members were all good first.

As Checkmate was getting ready to take a bath, she got a call from Karbonado. "What's up, Nado?" she asked.

"What's up, girl? What you doin'?"

"Nothin'. About to clean this kat."

"What? When you bought a cat?"

She burst out laughing. "Boy, I'm talkin' about washin' my ass!"

"Oh, okay. Tell me something, 'cause I thought you went and got a pet. Anyway, come open the door. I'm outside."

Checkmate sighed. "Damn, nigga, now is not the time." Rather than insist he wait, however, she said, "I'm on my way. Bye." She hung up the phone, smiling to herself as she walked to the front of the house. Checkmate always did have a thing for Karbonado, but out of love for her girls, she always dismissed the thought.

When she opened the door, Karbonado stood staring at her, unable to take his eyes of her body. She stood in front of him with nothing on but the towel wrapped around her.

"Nigga, is you just gonna stand there and lust on me or you comin' in?" she asked.

"Girl, please. Ain't nobody lustin'. You ain't got nothin' I wanna drool on!"

She giggled because she knew he was having sexual thoughts about her and was just trying to front.

He went straight to her couch and flopped down.

"Nigga, don't be floppin' on my shit like you live here! And get yo' feet off my table! Is you crazy?!"

Karbonado paid her no mind at all. All she could do was shake her head. She walked out of the living room and went to get in the tub of hot water she had already run, the scented bubbles giving the bathroom a smell of roses.

After relaxing in the tub for approximately five minutes, Karbonado walked into her bathroom butt ass naked.

When she noticed him, she started going off. "Nigga, get yo' ass out of here. You out of pocket and where the fuck is yo' clothes? You should be ashamed of yourself to have all that meat!" She was laughing by the time she finished yelling at him. She couldn't believe how bold he was to try her like she was some random female.

"Girl, shut up before yo' neighbor know my name."

She shook her head. She had always loved how he would just do shit with that boss attitude.

"Move so I can get in," he told her.

She slid up without another word and allowed him to get in the tub. Out of all the years she had known him, they had never done anything on that level. They had never kissed or even been in the same bed together.

Checkmate knew she was wrong, but shit. He had damn near forced her to let him get in the tub. At least that was what she kept telling herself.

Neither one of them said a word. They let Bob Marley and Lauryn Hill say everything that needed to be said: "Turn the light down low, right, right now. I want to give you some good, good lovin', right right now."

The mood was just right. Checkmate was really enjoying the moment they were sharing.

That was until she heard something very disturbing.

Brrrr, bloop, bloop.

Checkmate opened her eyes and turned around to face Karbonado. "You nasty son of a bitch! I can't believe you just farted in my water!"

"Our water," Karbonado said as if he had done nothing wrong.

She was so mad that she jumped out of the tub without drying her feet. As soon as her wet feet touched the tile, she slipped and fell on her ass. Karbonado laughed so hard he couldn't catch his breath. He got out of the tub and dried himself off. As soon as he made it to the room, Checkmate was getting ready to put her panties on. He walked up behind her.

"So you mad?" he asked.

"Karbonado, just leave me alone." Her voice was now calm.

"Man," he said and then slapped her on the ass. "Bitch, stop trippin'!" He had slapped her on the ass hard enough that she felt the sting in her pussy.

She turned around with her Glock 40 in her hand and pointed it at his head. "Nigga, if you would of been anybody else, I would pop yo' top. You better respect me. I don't give a fuck about you bein' my bestfriends' brother." She had fire in her voice.

Karbonado walked all the way up on her until the gun was touching his face. She couldn't believe how fearless he was. Most niggas bow down and beg for their life in the face of that heat. Instead, he grabbed her by the throat and caused her to rise up off of her feet. She was now holding the gun in his face while her tip toes jammed against the dresser behind her.

"Listen, bitch," Karbonado said while squeezing her neck tighter as he spoke, "I respect you, but I don't fear you. Pull the trigga, killer." He just stood there looking in her wide opened eyes for several seconds before he spoke again. "Pull the trigga, bitch! Don't ever think I'll be afraid of death." When nothing happened, Karbonado said, "Now get this gun out of my face!"

He slapped her, causing her to knock some stuff off of her dresser. She wanted to kill him so bad that she was shaking, but she was also turned on by how he had handled her. She had never allowed a man to treat her that way, but Karbonado was different.

Karbonado turned and got his things and left her house after he got dressed in the living room. He knew he was wrong for slapping her, but she needed to learn that a bitch was supposed to stay in her place. Had she have been anyone else, she would have been laying in a body bag.

CHAPTER 7

$$$

Two months after his trip to Miami, everything had been going as planned. Karbonado and his crew had the streets on lock. Money was coming in and niggas were jumping on the team. The Black Diamond Cartel had it one way: only niggas on the team eat.

This was Karbonado's everyday saying.

It was going down at Club Laboom on a Friday night. Lil Boosie was performing so everybody was trying to catch him live. Karbonado brought the whole team out and they flooded the entire top floor of in the VIP section.

The DJ was turned the fuck up and was giving shoutouts to the Black Diamond Cartel. The whole clique was feeling good, enjoying the weed and the bottles of expensive Champaign.

Rowdy and Lil Moma were dancing their asses off with some niggas. After twenty minutes of non-stop dancing, they went and took a seat. "Girl, these shoes killin' my feet!" Rowdy shouted while taking off her Christian Louboutin heels.

Karbonado just shook his head. He turned around when the girls started jumping because Checkmate hit the VIP section.

The girl was dressed to kill in her all white Givenchy dress and Giuseppe Zanotti heels. Niggas immediately started trying to shoot their shot, but couldn't hit the bullseye.

"Hey, Checkmate. Damn, I been missin' you." Both of the twins spoke at the same time as they often tended to do, as if they shared the same brain.

"I know. I just been busy tryin' to keep my foot on these niggas' neck." Right after she made the statement, she saw Karbonado. She looked at him and rolled her eyes as she got up and walked to the bar. She was still pissed at him.

She had never been mad at him for that long and had never gone for more than a day without talking to him at least once.

It had been two months.

Rowdy and Lil Moma noticed the sudden change in her and the fact that she and Karbonado didn't say a word to each other. They had also recognized that if one of them was around, the other one avoided the group. The girls didn't mention these unusual habits to either of them, but that didn't mean they didn't suspect that something was up between Karbonado and Checkmate.

Rowdy and Lil Moma got up and walked toward Checkmate.

"Girl, something is up with them two," Rowdy said.

Lil Moma put her two cents in as well. "Yeah, I been done noticed, but never said shit 'cause you know they always fightin' about something. I just figured they would get over it, but they ain't been around each other in months."

Checkmate was at the bar drinking Grey Goose mixed with Red Bull. She knew her friends peeped the tension between her and their brother, but she couldn't help it. She wanted to walk over and bust one of those bottles over his head. But she wasn't going to show her ass in public or in front of the other members of the cartel. Truth be told, she was afraid he would do what he had promised and kill her.

Lil Moma asked, "Girl, what's up? Why you all salty all of a sudden?"

Checkmate could tell she was really concerned, but she played it off. "Nothin'. It's just that time of the month," she lied.

The twins left it alone because they did understand how she got bitchy when she was on her period. They went back out on the dance floor and began dancing on each other like a pair of strippers, drawing stares from the men and women alike. Even getting a couple singles for their efforts. Rowdy saw Kaci and the girl that had been with her in the Gucci store. She walked up and greeted her. "Hey, girl, what's up!"

"Hey, girl, I see y'all came out to the Fourth of July party," Kaci said.

"Yeah, we just havin' a lil fun. My brother here. You wanna go holla at him in VIP?" Rowdy was loud even in the noise-filled club.

Kaci got a big smile on her face, "Yeah, I guess I could say hey."

Rowdy took Kaci and her friend up to the VIP area. Kaci was all smiles when she saw Karbonado. He was iced the fuck out and his demeanor screamed boss. She sat down next to him and talked for about twenty minutes. He had her cheesin' from ear to ear.

While Karbonado was talking to Kaci, his friend Damn Fool was talking to Kiara. Kiara was actually enjoying the conversation with Damn Fool. She knew he was a drug dealer because of the jewelry and expensive clothes he had on, but she decided for the first time not to judge. She simply tried to understand.

After talking to Damn Fool, Kiara gave him her phone number, and she and Kaci left the VIP section and went to watch Lil Boosie perform up close. Lil Boosie had the whole club rockin'. But before you knew it, the club was closing. Karbonado and his crew walked out of the club and headed to their cars. The parking lot looked like a car show. There was so many candy painted slabs on swangers, it was ridiculous.

Karbonado sat on his car and talked to a female from the Southwest. He had her wrapped in his arms until, out of the blue, someone snatched her by her hair and slung her to the ground.

"Bitch, beat ya feet!" Checkmate said.

Rowdy, Lil Moma, and the rest of the crew was surprised to see Checkmate do that, even though she regularly acted crazy. But no matter what, right or wrong, they were ridin' with her.

The girl looked at Checkmate then Karbonado. When she saw that he wasn't going to take up for her, she got up and left, feeling embarrassed.

After she was gone, Karbonado asked, "Checkmate, what the fuck wrong with you?"

"Let me tell yo' ass something, nigga. The next time you put yo' dick beaters on me, I'ma cremate them motherfuckas!" She turned to her best friends. "Rowdy, Lil Moma, y'all know I love you. But yo' brother better take my warning serious and keep his hands to hisself! I'm not playin' with his ass!"

After she was done yelling, Checkmate stomped off, but before she could take two steps, she was snatched by her hair.

Karbonado shocked everybody because they all knew Checkmate didn't make threats and not follow through on them.

"Listen, you had yo' chance to do what you wanted, but you didn't," Kardonado said. He pulled out his gun and pointed it at her head.

The crew was stunned and nervous, afraid he might pull the trigger. But Rowdy was the one who tried to take control of the situation. "Karbonado, have you lost yo' fuckin' mind? Get that fuckin' gun out her face!"

"Mind yo ' bizness, Rowdy," he said.

"Fuck you mean. This is my business!" Rowdy reached in her purse and grabbed a .357 and put it in his face. "Nigga, if you kill my friend, then I'll bury two people I love!" she said with tears streaming down her face. She hoped he didn't try her.

Karbonado saw it in her eyes. He knew she meant what she said. He put his gun down then looked Checkmate in the eyes, "We might as well get married, 'cause if I kill you, Rowdy will kill me. And if you kill me, Rowdy will kill you. So let's put this shit behind us." Karbonado kissed her on the lips right there in front of everyone.

They thought the whole thing had been crazy, but Checkmate shocked them even more with her words. "You right, but don't ever pull a gun on me again," she said before she kissed him back.

"You pulled a gun on me first so we even now," Karbonado reminded her.

By this time, Rowdy and Lil Moma started going crazy. "Oh, hell no! You two motherfuckas been fuckin' behind our backs?" The twins asked together.

"No!" Checkmate and Karbonado replied at the same time themselves.

Checkmate had to give them the real. "Look, we have never fucked. I would of at least told y'all." When the twins gave her that 'I know you lying' look, Checkmate smirked. "We were in the tub relaxin', listenin' to slow jamz. Everything felt right. I can't lie, I felt special. Y'all know I haven't been with nobody in a while. So things just felt right. The mood was set, and I honestly was gonna give him some—until he fucked up the mood!" She punched him in the arm playfully.

Rowdy asked, "What did he do?"

Checkmate looked at her friends and started giggling. "That nasty motherfucka farted while we were in the tub!"

Everybody began laughing, especially Rowdy with her loud behind, who was now laying on the ground and screaming.

"Karbonado, you wrong." Lil Moma told him.

"Then to make matters worse," Checkmate said, "that shit was funky! I was mad as hell!"

"So that's what started this whole fight?" Rowdy asked, damn near crying with laughter.

"See, she ain't tellin' y'all the whole story. The bitch call herself jumpin' out the tub with me, but she was so mad she forgot to dry her feet. As soon as she jumped out the tub, she crashed face first!"

Everybody started laughing all over again, and even Checkmate had to admit it was funny.

Karbonado wrapped his arms around her and kissed her. "I'll make it up tonight if you down," he promised her.

She smiled and walked to the passenger side of his car. She opened the door to get in, but the twins let her have it first. "You nasty bitch. I thought you was on yo' period?"

"I never said that," she said sweetly. "All I told you hoes was that it was that time of the month." She stuck up her middle finger and got in the car.

The twins shook their heads. They really didn't have a problem with Checkmate messing with their baby brother. She had been through so much, they wanted to see her happy, and if their brother was happy, too, then that was a double plus.

"Boy, bring yo' ass on," Checkmate told Karbonado. It had been some months since she got laid and tonight she was planning to give him the bizness.

Once Karbonado got in the car, he rushed to get home. He thought about the last time he saw Checkmate naked and got excited. As soon as he left the club parking lot, he stopped at the gas station. He wanted to sneak and pop a Viagra. He was planning to put in some serious work, and he had heard about Viagra boosting your stamina. He went into the store and popped the pill, paid for gas, and ran back to the car.

When he got back on the freeway, Checkmate decided to give him a little tease and herself some pleasure. She removed her shoes and placed her feet of the seat. She slid her dress up and cocked open her legs to play with her pussy.

Karbonado's dick got hard as a wrecking ball. He was having a hard time paying attention to the road.

"Damn, you need to hurry up and get to the house," she moaned. Checkmate continued to play with her pussy until she started cumin'. "Oh, shit I'm cummin!" She screamed and trembled as the orgasm shook her. "Oh, damn, that felt good," she said, closing her eyes in bliss.

Karbonado saw the juice on her fingers and sped up even more. He was damn near doing 100 mph on the beltway.

"Damn, nigga, slow down before you fuck around and kill our ass!" she yelled.

"Woman, just sit back and chill," he said, frustrated.

"What's the matter?" she asked. "Yo' lil man won't calm down?" Checkmate was now rubbing on his dick through his jeans. She started unbuckling his pants and pulled his dick out. She rubbed the head, pleased that his dick was so hard for her. Finally, she bent over to lick the pre-cum off the head. She kept licking around the tip of his dick until he swerved to the other lane.

"Boy, you need to stay yo' ass in the right lane before you wreck or get us pulled over," she said then started back to work on his dick. She was now sucking him like she was trying to win a dick sucking award. She sucked him until he started bustin' his load.

Once she was done, she put his dick back in his pants. "You owe me one, nigga. I don't mind givin', but I also wanna receive." Checkmate leaned back in her seat and closed her eyes until they arrived at the house.

Now it was time for Karbonado to show his skills. He picked her up and carried her all the way to the bedroom. After laying her on the bed, he raised up her dress and was surprised to find out that she didn't have on any panties. That turned him on even more.

He started tongue kissing her pussy. Checkmate was surprised at how good he worked his tongue. He sucked on her clit and flicked his tongue at the same time. She pushed his face deeper into her pussy. He pulled away, and she almost panicked thinking he was going to stop.

"Come ride my face," he told her. He laid on his back and allowed her straddle his face. At first, she rode slow, but as he began to devour her, she picked up speed. The next thing she knew, she was releasing a gallon of her juice all over his face.

Karbonado's face was soaking wet and her juice dripped from his face to the bed. Checkmate's whole body trembled as she screamed. After she came, she was drained and wanted to take a quick rest, but Karbonado had other plans. He got up and rolled her onto her stomach and spread her legs wide open. He pushed his dick in her and she sounded like she had taken her last breath. It had been a minute since she had some, and now here he was pushing his soul into her.

He began with slow, steady strokes, just making good love to her. He talked to her while working her walls in a circular motion. She was really enjoying hearing him tell her how good she felt and how her pussy belonged to him now. One thing she knew about him was that if he didn't mean it, he didn't say it.

Karbonado pulled out of her and made her lay on her back. He placed her legs over his shoulders, and when he put his dick in her this time, she tried to run. She scooted back so much she was now against the top of the bed with her feet crammed against the headboard. He was slamming his dick so deep into her, she thought he was gonna bust the bottom out of her pussy.

"Oooh, baby. Slow down. Oooh, yeah, right there. Right there. Damn, you ... know ... how ... to ... fuck ... a ... bitch. I'm cummin', baby! Shittt! Fuck, ooohhh, uhh." She screamed louder and louder as her eyes rolled in the back of her head, and Karbonado kept pounding like he was a sex machine.

After another ten minutes or so of jamming himself in and out of her, Karbonado started bustin' his load into her. "Uhh, damn, I'm nuttin'!" As he emptied himself, he slowed down, now drained by the phenomenal sex.

Checkmate was exhausted and didn't want to move. She just cuddled up to him and made up her mind that she wasn't going anywhere, and neither was he. She had never had a nigga that could put his foot down and put her in her place. And never had she been fucked so good.

After approximately thirty minutes of cuddling, Checkmate began to fall asleep. She was suddenly aroused by Karbonado growling in pain.

"What's up with you?" she asked still not moving.

"Ooh, shit. Damn, my shit hurtin'. He was in so much pain he was sweating.

Checkmate got up and turned the lights on. She noticed that his dick was still hard even though they had stopped fucking almost an hour earlier. "Nigga, I know you ain't been takin' Viagra!"

He was in so much pain all he could do was nod his head.

"Get yo' ass up so I can take you to the hospital," she told him.

"No! I ain't goin' nowhere like this. My shit won't go down!" Karbonado was more than a little scared now.

"Boy, get up. That's why yo' dumb ass need to go to the hospital! It ain't gonna go down on its own. Now put on some clothes and let's go!" Checkmate was mad as hell.

He got up and put his clothes on. When he was finally dressed, they were heading out the door but Karbonado stopped. He looked down at the bulge in his pants and was embarrassed. He didn't want to walk around with his manhood sticking out like that. He reached into his pants and lifted his dick up and placed it against his stomach. He tightened his belt up so that his dick would stay in place. Nobody would notice it because his shirt would cover it.

Checkmate wanted to laugh, but she held it in and walked to the car. "Nigga always fuckin' up a bitch mood," she mumbled to herself.

Karbonado got in the passenger seat and she drove to Kingwood hospital. Once they arrived and explained what was going on, the doctor gave him a shot. After twenty minutes, everything was back to normal. Karbonado just wanted to go home and relax, but the nurse gave him a bunch of paperwork to fill out.

"Man, this some bullshit. Damn, a nigga ready to go home and get some rest!"

Checkmate lost her temper. "Nigga, if you wouldn't've been taking those pills, we wouldn't be here! What, you can't fuck a bitch natural? You need Viagra like them 70-year-old men?"

"Baby, I didn't need it. It's just..." He paused. "It's just I wanted our first time to be special," he admitted to her.

"You call that special?" she questioned. "Fuckin' the shit outta me until you end up in the emergency room needin' a shot? What the fuck was so special about that? You always find a way to fuck up the mood!"

"Look, I fucked up, but at the same time, no matter how you look at it, I gave you a night to remember. How many niggas you been with fucked you good, then ended up in the emergency room? That's what I call puttin' in work!"

Checkmate could no longer hold back her laughter. "Boy, you is so stupid. Wait until I tell Rowdy about this shit!"

Karbonado laughed with her.

By the time he was finished with all of the paperwork, it was late. They left the hospital and went back to the house and went to sleep. Checkmate enjoyed sleeping in his bed. She felt that it was now made only for two people: him and her.

CHAPTER 8

$$$

Karbonado woke up the next morning smelling food cooking. He got out of bed, brushed his teeth, then walked into the kitchen. Checkmate was at the stove cooking, looking so sexy in nothing but his wife beater. He walked up behind her and kissed her on the neck.

"Umm. It's about time you got up, Mr. Viagra," she joked.

"Oh, yeah," Karbonado responded. He bent her over and slid his dick into her. She was so wet you could hear her juices smacking every time he took a stroke.

"Oooh yess, give it to me," she moaned. He started beating her pussy and she tried to run. But he wouldn't let her. She tried to tell him to lighten up. "Oooh, baby, hold up. Waittt. Damn! Baby, you might tear somethin'." She kept moaning. "Oooh, you must be on Viagra! Oooh, I'm cummin'! I'm cummin', baby!"

Karbonado started pounding fast as he could. She was out of breath and couldn't get anymore words out. "Ahh, I'm cummin'" he cried out as his legs begin to buckle. He was falling and refused to fall by himself.

They both fell down and was on the floor laughing. "Damn. Why you pull me down?"

"'Cause I wasn't about to fall and listen to you laugh at me, so here we are. Laughin' together." He was breathing hard. "Plus, that was for that Viagra slug you shot!"

Karbonado got up and helped Checkmate up. They got themselves together and ate breakfast. After they were done eating, they decided to lay in bed and watch movies all day. While they were watching *Jason's Lyric*, Checkmate's phone rang.

She looked at it and saw that it was Jania. She smiled, very happy to hear from the girl. "Hello," Checkmate answered.

"Hey, Checkmate, umm," Jania paused for a second. "Checkmate, can you come and get me?" she asked, her voice making it obvious that she was crying.

"What's wrong, Nia, and where you at?"

"I'm at Northline Mall at the bus stop. Can you please just come get me?"

"I'm on my way, Jania. Give me about 20 minutes to get out of the bed and get dressed and get there. Are you by yo'self?"

Jania told her, "Yeah, I'm by myself."

"Look, go inside the mall and wait on me. I'm on the way. I'll call you back when I get there." Checkmate got up and hurriedly got dressed. She gave Karbonado a short version of Jania's call then kissed him before she headed out the door.

Checkmate had promised Jania that if she ever needed her, all she had to do was call. She was not about to let her down. She knew how it felt to need somebody and not have anyone. She knew what it felt like to be alone.

She was on 59 headed north, driving way over the speed limit. What she said would be 20 minutes, turned into 14. When she got to the mall, she called Jania. "I'm outside. Just come out through the Magic Johnson Theater and you will see a white BMW 750."

After a minute went by, Jania came out of the front door of the theater. She had on some clothes that were dingy and flip flops, and she was carrying a small backpack.

Checkmate couldn't stand the sight of her looking so damn homeless. She opened the door, got in, and put her backpack on the floor.

Jania had a black eye.

"Nia, what happened to yo' eye?" she asked in a soft, caring tone.

Jania started crying.

Checkmate rubbed her back. "It's okay, Nia. You don't have to tell me right now. Just let it out and talk to me when you ready."

Checkmate was going to take Jania to her house. After she had been driving for five minutes, she realized that she needed to go back by Karbonado's spot. When she rushed out of the house, she had forgotten to get her purse. All she had grabbed was her phone and car keys. It was a habit to always carry $5,000 and two guns in her console just in case she needed it.

"Nia, when the last time you ate?" Checkmate asked.

Jania put her head down and thought for a second. "Around five yesterday."

She didn't say anything, but stopped at Popeye's and ordered a bunch of food for her, Jania, and Karbonado. "What you want to drink?"

"Um, strawberry," Jania answered.

After getting their food, they pulled off and went to the house. When Checkmate got to the gate, she pushed the button and the gate opened. Jania's eyes got wide as hell. She had never seen or been around houses that big.

"Is this where you live?" she asked in awe.

Checkmate laughed. "No, this is my boyfriend's house," she said pointing at Karbonado's place. "And those two houses over there are my best friends' houses, who are my boyfriend's sisters. And that house over there is their father's house, but he dead." She pulled up into Karbonado's driveway. "Come on," she told Jania as she got out of the car.

When they got to the porch, Checkmate unlocked the door and they went inside. Jania was stuck in a trance as she entered the house.

"Baby!" Checkmate called out. She walked around the house and saw that he wasn't there. "Nia, you can come in here, but take yo' shoes off before steppin' on this carpet," she warned.

Jania did as she was instructed while Checkmate set the food out on the table. They both washed their hands at the kitchen sink then sat down to eat. Jania soon realized that she had eaten half of the food by herself and was embarrassed that she had eaten more than Checkmate.

"Checkmate, I'm so sorry," she said, once again her head bowed in shame.

"Sorry about what?" Checkmate asked.

"I didn't mean to eat so much. It's just, the food was so good." Tears ran down her face.

Checkmate lifted her chin up and wiped her tears with a napkin. "Nia, I'm not trippin' on this shit. You hungry, then eat until you full."

"Thank you," Jania said. She was still a little self-conscious, but she started tearing up the rest of the chicken.

Checkmate started chuckling. "I thought my fat ass could eat, but damn!" Jania began to laugh too.

After watching Jania eat 12 pieces of chicken, Checkmate decided to ask some questions. "So are you gonna tell me what's wrong? And what happened to yo' eye?"

Jania reached up and touched her eye gently. She waited a full minute before she said anything. "Checkmate, please don't judge me when I tell you this," she said, tears beginning to slide down her cheeks again.

"Nia, come on. I will never judge you. Tell me what's wrong."

"Well, my granny died a month ago. So I was forced to live with my mother. The thing about my mother is she's a dope fiend. That's why my granny took me in. All my mom care about is her next high. I barely would see her and we never had food in the house. At first, it didn't matter because I had the money you gave me. Well, some of it. But that money went away fast because I was buying food and catching the bus to school everyday.

"Two weeks after living with my mom, all the money was gone. One day my mom came home with some Burger King, and I was so happy until I found out she only brought food for herself. She sat in my face and ate everything she bought. When I asked her why she didn't bring me something, she told me closed legs don't get fed.

"I ended up crying myself to sleep that night. All I could think about was how my granny always made sure I ate. I thought about the nights Granny didn't eat just to make sure I did. I thought about the time when Granny had one dollar, and she went to McDonald's and got me a burger. I tried to split it with her, but she told me she was alright as long as I got to eat something." She paused. "Today, I was walking down Jensen, trying to figure out how I could get something to eat. While I was walking, this old man, about 60 years old, pulled over and asked if I wanted to make some money. I told him I don't sell my body.

'Then why you on the hoe stroll?' he asked me. I explained that my house was down the block, and he said, 'Well, you don't have to sell your body to get paid.' He told me he only wanted to watch me twerk and he would pay me $200. All I had to do was dance to five of his favorite songs. So I agreed to go to his house.

"I didn't want to dance for no money, I swear I didn't. But I was so hungry. It had been two days since I ate anything. Once I got to his house, I danced for him. He had me dance to some old Barry White song. But I danced no matter how trashy the song was. After I finished the five songs, I asked for my money. He gave me the money and then offered me $500 more to have sex with him, and I told him no.

"That's when he started yelling at me and calling me bitches and stupid hoes. Anything you can think of, he called me that. I asked him to drop me back at where he picked me up from, and he told me no. Then he asked for his money back and I told him no, that I had earned it. And that's when he punched me in the eye and went in my pants pocket and took the money back. I ended up giving that punk a free dance. After I walked to the bus stop, that's when I called you."

By the time she finished telling about her ordeal, Jania was sobbing, and Checkmate had a face full of tears as well. "Nia, why you didn't call me like I told you to? Why did you wait so long?"

Jania said, "Because I was ashamed. I didn't know how to tell you I had a place to stay but nothing to eat. Plus, you had already helped me when you didn't even know me." She was crying so hard now that she hiccupped.

"I understand, Nia. Don't cry. I got you from this day forward. I will protect you and provide for you like you're my daughter. You can live with me and you'll never go without a meal again. All you got to do is go to school, make good grades, and graduate. Is that too much to ask for?"

"No, I will do everything you ask. How could I turn you down when all you ever did was help me? I will go to school and graduate." Jania meant these promises with all of her heart.

62

Checkmate reached out to her and Jania walked into her arms. She hugged the girl with all she had and said, "Okay, now do you remember where that nigga stay?" Her voice was soft, but there was no mistaking the anger that she felt.

"Yeah, he lived in a blue and white house by the Ice Cream Castle on Airline," she replied.

"Good. Now go put yo' shoes on so we can pay this old motherfucka a visit." Her voice held that aggressiveness that was her trademark.

Jania was afraid, but she did what she was told. Checkmate was about to spill blood. It was one thing she couldn't stand, and that was a man like the one Jania had described.

CHAPTER 9

$$$

Detective Carter and Detective Moore had been trying to get a lead on this female killer. After investigating the people in Garden City they learned that it was a female that killed Young Hogg's brother and sister. The two detectives couldn't believe what witnesses explained to them.

"How could a woman kill two people the way she did, then threaten to kill a baby?" Detective Carter shouted.

"I don't know, but we need to get her off the streets because it's no telling how many more bodies she got under her belt," Detective Moore stressed.

While they were at the office, they had a visitor. "How you doing, Kiara Washington?" Detective Carter asked.

"I'm doing fine. I was getting ready to head home. I just wanted to say bye before I leave."

"Okay, you make sure you drive safe and be careful. We got a serial killa out there somewhere," he said with a laugh.

When she left the office, Detective Carter spoke his mind.

"Do you know one of our officers saw her at Club Laboom?" he asked.

"Okay, what's wrong with that?" she questioned.

"She was seen with Kaci Conner, the lawyer that represented Jason Lewis, Jr. They were in the VIP with him, partying and laughing. The officer said that Kaci and Jason may have a lil something going on with each other."

"So you think Kiara might be dirty?"

"I'm not sure, but I'm just looking at the fact that her best friend represented a killer and now they're just hanging in VIP. I know Jason is dirty. We just have to prove it, and I think I have the perfect idea." The detective had a big grin on his face.

*****

Checkmate had just pulled up outside of the house Jania told her the old man lived. She was trying to figure out a plan to get in the house without alarming him. After a quick thought, she had the perfect plan.

"Look, Nia, stay in the car. When I call yo' phone, then come in."

She made sure Jania understood her orders then Checkmate walked up to the house.

After knocking on the screen a few times, the old man that Jania described answered the door.

Checkmate said, "Hi, my name is Kelly. My car broke down up the street and I was wondering if you could help me out?" There was a hint of desperation in her voice. It was also clear that Checkmate could speak proper grammar when she chose to.

"Yeah, sure, come on in for a minute. Let me get my keys and tools."

Once she walked into the house, she asked to use the restroom. He told her it was down the hall. "Thank you," she said in a pleasant tone. Inside the bathroom, she called Jania and said, "Hey, come in the house in exactly two minutes."

After Jania confirmed that she understood, Checkmate hung up the phone and flushed the toilet. When she got back to the front room, the old man was smiling. "Are you ready to see what's wrong with your car, pretty lady?" He was doing his best to charm her.

"Um, yeah, let's do it," she said, reaching in her purse and pulling out a 9mm. She now had it aimed at his face. The old man's eyes became as big as golf balls. "Sit yo' bitch ass down!"

"Pretty lady, please don't kill me. If you need money I have plenty. Just don't kill me!" He begged like the coward he was.

By this time, he noticed the front door open. He could not believe that it was the same young girl that he had hit earlier and had taken the money from.

"Nia, come here," Checkmate told her. Jania was scared because she never expected Checkmate to go this far. "Do you remember her, motherfucka?"

The man couldn't talk fast enough and that was his second mistake. She shot him in his left foot.

Boom!

She shot him in the other foot.

"Ahhh! Fuck! Damn it!" He just screamed curse words over and over.

"I asked you a fuckin' question. Now keep tryin' me and I'll blow yo' fuckin' nose off!"

"Yes, I remember her and I'm sorry!" he yelled.

Jania was scared as hell. She had never seen anybody get shot in front of her before.

"Where's the money you promised her then took back?" When he looked shocked, she said, "Yeah, don't look surprised. She told me the whole story, you sick motherfucka!"

Boom!

She shot him in the left hand.

"Ahhh! Please, stop! Please, stop! The money is in that jar on top of the shelf! You can have it all, just please leave!" Now he was the one shedding tears.

"Nia, go get that money!" she shouted. Jania did what she was told. "How much is it?"

"Seventy five hundred," the old man cried. "Please, just take it and go." He was blowing snot, and tears streamed down his face.

"Nia, come here," Checkmate called. Jania went to her, and that's when Checkmate went ape. She shoved the gun in his mouth, breaking his front teeth. "You said he tried to get you to let you fuck, right?" Jania nodded her head yes. "Come grab this gun!" she ordered. Jania stood frozen with fear. "I'm not gonna repeat myself, Nia."

Jania grabbed the gun from her. Her hand was shaking so bad she could barely hold on to the heavy pistol.

"Nia, this man did you dirty. He made you lower yo' standard and do something you didn't want to do. Now if you want yo' revenge, then pull that trigger and let's go. Or if you want him to hunt you down and try to hurt you later, then don't pull the trigger and let's go."

"I can't do it," she said and gave Checkmate the gun. "I'm sorry, I can't do it." She began to cry, hating that she was disappointing Checkmate.

"It's okay, Nia. I'm not mad at you. But he gonna die today, and I'm gonna be the one to pull the trigga. You probably not the first, but you the last person he's gonna hurt. Now go outside and get in the car. And here…take this money too."

Once Jania was gone, she had a few words for the old man.

"You nasty motherfucka, you don't deserve to live!"

She shot six times.

"I can't stand motherfuckas like you!" she yelled then spit on him.

When she got back to the car, Jania was looking scared as hell. Checkmate stared at her, eyes full of sympathy. "Listen, no matter what, don't think I'm mad at you and don't be mad at me. I just have no tolerance for men like him." She put the car in gear and drove off.

After pulling back into Karbonado's driveway, she cut the engine and they got out and walked into the house to find him laying on the couch watching his favorite movie *Belly*. Checkmate had to tell him to put some clothes on because he was only wearing a pair of boxers. He looked at Jania and apologized.

"It's okay," she said. "This is your house."

He walked to his bedroom to put some clothes on.

"Nia," Checkmate said to her in a very serious voice, "no matter what, don't ever talk about what happened at that house to nobody."

Jania understood the seriousness behind the warning. "I promise. I'll never mention anything. Oh yeah, here." She tried to hand Checkmate the money they got from the house.

"No, I don't need it. It's yours to do whatever you want. Tomorrow, I will take you shoppin', and I'll enroll you in a new school."

Jania couldn't hold back her tears. She grabbed Checkmate and hugged her so tight that she couldn't breathe.

"Damn, Nia, I can't breathe!" They both started laughing through their tears.

"Thanks for everything," Jania said.

Checkmate really loved how she was able to bring a little joy into this little girl's life who had already experienced way more pain than any child should ever have to. She knew how it felt to need or want

68

someone in your life that really cared about what happened to you. And she promised herself that she would change Jania's lifestyle for the better.

*****

Karbonado was in the room putting on clothes as he wondered who the young girl that Checkmate brought home was. He figured that she had to be someone that was kin to her because Checkmate wasn't the type to bring just anybody around him or his family.

Checkmate came in the room and answered the question that was on his mind. "Baby, Jania will be staying with us from now on."

"Stayin' with us?" he asked a little shocked. "Since when did you start stayin' here? Matter fact, you ain't even gotta answer that." He walked into the living room. "Excuse me, baby girl. What's yo' name?"

Jania smiled and said, "Jania, and thanks for letting me live with y'all."

"Baby girl, we'll talk about that in a second. Let me show you around." He grabbed her hand, pulled her off the couch, and led her around the coffee table to his room. Pointing at all of the clothes in his closet, he said, "Baby girl, look at this. All this expensive shit is fit for a king." Then he walked her to the bathroom and pointed to all the different cologne, picking up different bottles and allowing her to smell them. She was impressed with his taste. "This is the right smell for a king," he said, then walked her to the dresser. "You see, this is the top of the line underwear, made just for the king.

"Now, I'm showing you this so you can see. Whatever dream she sold you about stayin' here, get that out yo' mind, 'cause she don't even stay here. I just showed you ain't shit here but king shit. Now get out!"

69

Jania was so embarrassed she ran out of the room without saying a word.

"You stupid son of a bitch!" Checkmate yelled as she ran out of the door to get Jania.

Jania was standing by Checkmate's car, and it hurt to see that the girl was crying because of Karbonado. "Nia," she told her, "I am so sorry. Please don't hate me. I told you I will take care of you and I meant that. Fuck Karbonado. That nigga ass be on some bullshit sometimes. Come on. I'ma take you by my best friends' house.

"Checkmate, can we just go to your house? I don't want to meet anybody else." The girl looked so ashamed it was pitiful.

Checkmate felt so bad for her. Jania had been through enough embarrassment for one day, and Checkmate was not about to let her down again. "Okay, let's go," she told Jania.

They got in Checkmate's BMW and went to her place.

CHAPTER 10

$$$

Kiara thoroughly enjoyed the past three hours. She had received a call from Damn Fool, and he convinced her to meet him at Deerbrook Mall. They were in the food court really feelin' each other.

"So how did you get the nickname Damn Fool?" Kiara asked.

"Because my mama raised a damn fool!" he said.

Kiara spat out some of her drink from laughing so hard.

"You alright?" Damn Fool asked while taking a napkin and wiping her drink off the side of her mouth.

"Yeah, but you wrong for making me laugh like that," she told him.

"I can tell you really haven't smiled much. What's up with that?"

She wanted to reveal who she really was, but she was enjoying him so much that she didn't want to run him off. "I do laugh, but I just haven't been around nobody that's actually funny lately. I mean, you should try standup."

"Oh, so now you take me for a joke?" he asked, a little offended.

She noticed that his mood had changed and she felt the need to clear things up. "No, I don't take you for a joke. I really believe that you could do standup. Your jokes are really funny. I'm the type that won't laugh if I don't think something is funny."

He calmed down and thought about what she said. "You could be right. I never thought about no shit like that."

"I got a friend who owns a comedy club called Just Jokin'. If I got you on set, would you do it?"

He thought about it some more and was really getting intrigued now. He really wasn't interested in getting on stage as much as he was interested in impressing her and getting in her pants. He agreed to do it. "Yeah, I'll do it, but the owner gotta promise not to laugh at my jokes."

She couldn't control herself. She really believed that he could do standup and become something.

Things were cool and they were having fun—until Brianna walked up.

"Nigga, how you gonna play me like I'm just some jump off? Your son needs shoes and I need some money for bills." His baby mama held out her hand like she was running something.

He reached into his pocket and pulled out $1,200 and handed it to her. "Here, take this and go buy you a new attitude. You know damn well that I just gave you money yesterday, and he got enough shoes to last three years."

Brianna counted the money and wasn't satisfied. "Nigga, this ain't shit. I can't even pay my rent with this!" She was being ghetto loud.

Damn Fool went back in his pocket and pulled out another $500. "Here, now leave me alone. Don't ask me for nothin' else." She took the money, rolled her eyes then looked at Kiara and told her, "Don't get too comfortable. I don't share his money with nobody but my son.

72

If he start missin' payments, then I'ma put them laws in his life. And it's hard to sell drugs when the cops watchin' you." She rolled her neck, turned around, and walked off.

Damn Fool was so pissed and embarrassed with the way Brianna had just acted. "Kiara, I'm sorry about that. My baby mama is silly," he said.

"Look, it's cool," she said, "but I need to know if you still mess with her. And, please, be honest with me."

"No!" he said with conviction. "My son is our only connection and that's what she use to get her way."

Kiara's voice got softer. "So is it true? What she said about you selling drugs?" She really hoped that he would say it wasn't true.

"Look, Kiara. I don't really know you, but I like you enough to be honest. I hope that don't change how you view me. I been on my own since I was 15. My mama passed and I don't know any of my family because my mom is from New York. I've been in Houston all of my life. I never wanted to be a drug dealer, but it seemed to be my only way to survive." His confession was honest and sincere.

This made Kiara like him even more. She actually felt his pain and wanted to help him be more than a drug dealer. "I don't look at you different, but I'm not gonna tell you that I agree with your choices. Just do me one favor."

"What's that?" he asked.

"When I get you on the set at Just Jokin' Comedy Club, give it your all. I believe you will really make the crowd laugh."

They stared at each other for a moment before he said, "I got you, but this club better be worth my jokes."

*****

73

It was 10:00AM and Checkmate was in a dead sleep until the smell of food woke her up. She got up and found Jania in the kitchen cooking her ass off.

"Damn, it smell good, Nia. What you cookin'?"

"Eggs, bacon, biscuits, and hash browns. But you ain't gettin anything until you brush your teeth." Jania covered her nose with her hand.

Checkmate laughed, then left to go take care of herself. After ten minutes, she was back in the kitchen trying to eat. While making her plate, her phone started ringing. She looked at the phone and was about to ignore the call but decided against it.

"What the fuck do you want?" she yelled. "I can't believe you trippin' with me!"

Karbonado told her to calm down, which only made her madder. "Look, nigga, you ain't gotta worry about us. We good. You was wrong for sayin' and doin' what you said and did!" Checkmate hung up the phone, not even giving him a chance to get a word in.

After they ate, she told Jania to go pick out an outfit from her closet. The girl was smiling from ear to ear when she saw all of the expensive clothes. She had never had anything that wasn't off the clearance rack. Jania picked out an all-white Gucci sweat suit and some white Gucci loafers. She felt like a superstar at that moment.

Checkmate walked into the room and smiled at Jania making different poses in the mirror. "Are you ready, Miss America?" she asked, smiling.

"Yeah, I'm ready."

They got in the car and drove to the Galleria. Checkmate took her to every store and allowed her to have whatever she wanted.

Jania had never been this happy in her life. She was living like a princess. It wasn't the fact that she was getting a bunch of stuff, but the fact that someone cared enough to get her anything at all. "Checkmate, can I get something for my three friends?" she asked.

"Yeah, you can get them one thing each. Then it's time to go 'cause we goin' to get yo' nails done and yo' hair. Plus, tomorrow, I'm enrolling you in school." It really touched Checkmate's heart that even after everything that had happened to Jania the last few months with her grandmother dying, a pervert hurting her, and Karbonado acting a fool, she was still thinking about other people.

Jania got her three friends a Gucci backpack each, one white, one black, and the last one pink. They would really appreciate her getting each of them their favorite color.

After the shopping trip and getting her hair and nails done, she was tired and ready to take a nap. The excitement had worn her out. But Checkmate wanted to stop by Rowdy and Lil Moma's place.

"Nia, I want you to meet the twins. I promise you will love them and they not like that asshole you met last night."

After all Checkmate had done for her, she wouldn't dare tell her no. Because not one time did Checkmate tell her no. "Okay, I'm cool with that," she said and closed her eyes to take a quick nap.

*****

Rowdy and Karbonado were in the game room shooting pool. They had been gambling for the past hour. Lil Moma was watching and playing bartender.

Checkmate had her own key, so she just walked into the house. She could hear everybody upstairs in the game room so she and Jania went upstairs.

"Hey, y'all" Checkmate said.

The girls ran and hugged her. "Hey, girl, where yo' ass been? And who is this pretty girl you got with you?" As usual Rowdy was happy and was excited to see them.

"This is my girl Jania, and she my lil sidekick," she said as she made eye contact with Karbonado. "And she's the 15-year-old girl Karbonado kicked out last night." She was still pissed.

"What?" the twins asked, staring at their baby brother.

"Man, don't bring yo' ass up in here with that petty shit. You know the rules. You know how I am about new people around me." He was trying to act like he wasn't wrong.

"Nigga, she's a kid. How dare you do that to her?! You were wrong, Karbonado. I ride with you on a lot of things, but that was wrong!" Now Rowdy was pissed at him too.

"What I'm trippin on," Checkmate began, "is how you had the nerves to fuck the shit out of me last night, then the next day tell me I can't stay there. Like I'm one of yo' jump offs. Nigga, you got me fucked up, and you better stop playin' with my emotions before yo' sisters have to bury me and ya' ass!"

Karbonado sighed then said, "How you think I feel? You fuck me last night, get up and leave, skip the pregnancy, then come back to the house with some crumb snatcher, talkin' about she stayin' with us. No, she's not!" He was still acting a damn fool.

Smack!

Checkmate slapped him so hard that he had to ask about it.

"Rowdy, did this bitch just slap me?" he asked, stunned that they were doing this again.

"Hell, yeah, she slapped yo' stupid ass!" Rowdy replied.

"Damn, that's how it is, Checkmate?" he asked.

"Look, nigga, I was this little girl at one point. I know what it is to not have a safe place to live, and guess who opened they arms? It was

Rowdy and Lil Moma! I didn't change or forget where I came from 'cause I have money now." Checkmate had tears in her eyes.

"Jania, come here," he called. She looked at the girls and they nodded to let her know she was okay. He opened his arms, then hugged her. "I'm sorry, Jania. I know I been a asshole. Will you forgive me?"

She hugged him back. "I forgive you," she told him.

"Checkmate, come here," he said after he released Jania.

She came to him and he kissed her. "I'm sorry for everything I said. You know how I be trippin' sometimes. If y'all gonna move in, then I'm down with it." He looked at her and smiled. "We could use a maid."

Everybody laughed.

Jania was having the best day. She felt like she finally had a family again, and she wasn't about to do anything to mess that up.

Later that night, she was in her new room writing in her tablet. Jania knew how to write music, but not too many people realized that except for her three best friends. Karbonado had promised that he would buy her everything she wanted to put in her room. She loved how he had gone from being heartless to somebody with a gigantic heart.

While writing a verse, she heard someone knocking on her door. "Come in," she told them.

"What you doin', Nia?" Checkmate asked.

"Nothing, just writing my thoughts. Why, what's up?"

"Oh, I was gettin' ready to go to sleep, and I just wanted to make sure you was alright. How do you like yo' room so far?"

Jania's eyes widened with happiness. "Well, it's bigger than my granny's old apartment. So I'm blessed, and Karbonado said he would get me whatever I wanted for my room." She was full of barely contained joy. Checkmate was surprised and glad he was now acting like he had sense. There was no way she was going to continue to let him treat Jania like he had starting out.

*****

"I need a favor, Sean," Kiara told her cousin.

"What's up, Kiara? You still ain't paid me for the last favor."

"Boy, shut up. How many times I kept your ass from goin' to jail? How many times did you get pulled over and used my name to get off the hook?" Kiara was a little irritated that she had to remind him because she seldom asked for anything.

"Alright, alright! What do you need?"

"I have a friend," she began, though it was obvious from the way she said it that the dude was more than a friend, "that needs a shot at the next standup. I prefer you let him open up for you. I'm telling you, this man is funny as hell."

"I don't know. You know I can't just give anybody an opening act when I have never heard of them. But I'll tell you what, I usually pay $1200 for an open act. But since you vouching for this dude, I will only pay him if the crowd doesn't boo him. I'll write all of that in his contract. That's the best I can do. Make sure he's on time. He will open up in three weeks for Mike Epps. So come by in two days so he can sign the contract."

That was really more than she was hoping for. She really believed that Damn Fool would become a star doing comedy.

CHAPTER 11

$$$

"Ahhh! Come on, man. I'm tellin' you the truth!" Lil Ronnie could take much more of this pain.

Young Hogg had him tied up and was beating him damn near to death. "So you tellin' me you work for Karbonado, but don't know a thing about his whereabouts?" Young Hogg yelled.

"We don't deal with him direct. We answer to Checkmate, and she only come around once a month. But when she do, she's guarded very heavy!" Lil Ronnie was snitching like there was no tomorrow. And for him, there probably wouldn't be.

Young Hogg could understand this. None of his workers knew where he lived, nor did they have direct contact with him. He pulled out his phone and dialed the number that Lil Ronnie gave him.

Checkmate answered on the third ring. "What's up? Who this?"

"Bitch, you think I'm gonna let you kill my lil sister and brother and not do shit? You just get ready for a funeral." He placed the phone to Lil Ronnie's ear, and said, "Talk, nigga!"

"Checkmate, please help me!" Lil Ronnie cried out in terror. "Don't let me die like this!"

Checkmate hated to see him in the position he was in, but was life in the game. "Lil Ronnie, you know I always kept it real with you. And I'm not gonna change that. You was a good soulja, now die one!" Her words surprised the Garden City Cartel and Young Hogg.

Young Hogg had to admit that he had never met a bitch as ruthless as Checkmate.

He shot Lil Ronnie repeatedly, unable to control his anger. He had been looking for them relentlessly and couldn't seem to make anybody talk. Plus, he wanted to break Checkmate, and maybe that just wasn't going to happen.

"Bitch, I'll catch you slippin'!" he yelled into the phone, hoping it was true.

Once he looked at the screen, he noticed that she had hung up the phone 30 seconds earlier. He faced every member of the Garden City Cartel. "I want that bitch right here! I want everybody that's affiliated with her and the Black Diamond Cartel dead! I'm willing to pay $500,000 to whoever bring her to me, and another $500,000 for Karbonado."

*****

Karbonado was listening to Checkmate explain what Young Hogg had just done.

"I should of just killed that punk ass niece of his. I can't lie. It bothered me hearin' Lil Ronnie beg for my help. I had to treat him like an outsider. I mean, baby, we both know that he was dead. There was no way Young Hogg would let him live." She was feeling bad that someone in her crew died thinking that she didn't care.

"Baby, that's part of the game. He tried to use Ronnie to get to us, but it didn't work. Now it's our time to strike back. I got a plan, but we gonna need to catch a few of his boyz and make 'em an offer they can't refuse. We need to get them to give us some good info on him or his family.

"This time." He pause for several seconds, then continued. "Not only will we kill a family member, but we will air out the funeral." Karbonado smiled, and it wasn't a happy smile.

"Baby, we got to protect Nia. I know you wasn't feelin' me just poppin' up with her, but I'm all she got. We all she got. I don't know what it is, but it's something about her that would not allow me to walk away. I mean she's really a good kid and I want to see her become more than what we are."

This was one of the few times he had truly seen her express herself with emotion. Softly and with tenderness in his eyes, he said, "I understand, bae. I have grown to like her too, and you have my word I'll make sure she's protected." He didn't often make promises, but when he did he meant every word.

While they were talking, Jania knocked on the door. "Come in," Checkmate told her. She opened the door and ran, taking a dive on the bed. "Girl, why is you jumping on my bed?" Checkmate asked, laughing.

"What are y'all doing?" Jania asked excitedly.

"Nothin', Nia. What's up? And why you all excited?"

"Um, I just got off the phone with Cupcake, Cornbread, and Darkskin," she said shyly. She still had a hard time asking for things. "Next week, we plan on meeting up at Deerbrook Mall. That's if it's okay with y'all?" She was really hoping that they didn't say no, which is something they had not done yet. But she did not want to take advantage of them in any way.

81

"Yeah, you can go, but we not leaving you by yo'self. We not gonna try to invade yo' privacy, but we will do some shoppin' and catch a movie." With that clown Young Hogg out there, Checkmate planned on keeping a close look out for Nia.

"That's cool," Jania said, happy as she could be. "We wanted to go see that new movie, *Soul Man.*"

Karbonado just shook his head. That girl got so excited over the simplest things. "So," he said, "I guess we gotta pick them girls up too?"

"No, Cupcake's boyfriend is going to bring them up there," Jania answered.

"Here." Karbonado handed Jania the keys to his Range Rover and Checkmate's BMW. She looked at him confused. "Take yo' butt out there and wash our cars. That will be yo' job for this week." He was smiling, but serious about teaching her some responsibility.

She took the keys and ran outside to do what he asked. She always got whatever she wanted, and they would only make her do small stuff around the house, like keeping the place clean, doing the laundry, and washing the cars. Their number one rule was that she had to go to school, bring home As and Bs, and stay out of trouble. And because she did everything they asked without complaint or delay, she always got $500 a week as an allowance.

Jania had been going to her new school, Nimitz High, for three days, and a lot of girls were jealous of her because she had all of the top notch designer clothes. She never acted like she was better than anyone else, but because she didn't hang out with many people or talk much, they took it as being stuck up. The truth was that she was very shy when it came to meeting new people.

As she was standing outside the next day, waiting on Karbonado to pick her up, this twelfth grader named Glen approached her. "What's up, sexy. Can I get your number? Maybe I can take you out?" As he was speaking, he pulled out a knot of money, trying to impress her.

"Look, I don't mean to sound rude, but can you please not flash your money at me? I'm not for sale, nor can your money buy me a pair of Gucci socks."

"Bitch, you ain't all that. I got plenty girls dyin' for me to take them out." He stuck out his chest like an angry little boy.

"Look, it's obvious that you don't know who my daddy is. But I'ma pretend like I never heard you call me a bitch." She looked him in the eye, but he was too stupid to see the warning.

"I don't give a fuck who yo' daddy is!" he yelled.

"Okay, we will see. Matter of fact, here he is now. Just hold that thought." She laughed. This fool didn't have a clue.

When she made it to the truck, she got in with a frown on her face. "What's wrong with you?" Karbonado asked.

She pointed at Glen, and told him, "That boy called me a bitch. Then after I told him I'ma pretend like I didn't hear that and that it was obvious he didn't know who my daddy was, he said he didn't give a fuck who you was."

He smiled. "So now I'm supposed to get out of the car and play the daddy role?"

"Uh, duh!" she said, laughing.

Karbonado got out of the truck and walked right up to Glen, pulling his gun out. "So it's fuck me, lil nigga?" he growled.

"Uhhh, I, I, I was just playin'. I'm sorry!" He was so scared, he was stuttering like he had a speech impediment.

Karbonado waived Jania over, and she got out of the truck, walking over to stand next to him. "Nigga, you better tell my daughter you sorry, or I'll blow yo' shit back right here!" he yelled for everybody to hear.

"I'm sorry!" he cried out. "I'm sorry!"

All of the students saw what was going on and started laughing because Glen was always bullying people.

"Good. Now listen to me real good. You better not fuck with my baby ever in life. And you better warn yo' lil homies, too. 'Cause I'm gonna hold you responsible. Do you got that?" Karbonado was snarling by the time he finished.

"Yes, yes, I'll spread the word!" he cried.

"Let's go, Nia," Karbonado demanded.

She was about to follow him, but she stopped and reached in her pocket. Nia pulled out a $50 bill. "Here, go buy yourself some Pampers. You too old to be running around shittin' on yourself!" Again, everybody in the parking lot laughed at Glen. Nia made it to the truck, but had one more question for him. "Who's the bitch now?" she asked laughing.

From that point on, she had no problems when it came to boys disrespecting her. Most boys were scared to even speak. The funny thing about the whole situation was that Karbonado never even had a clip in the pistol. He only wanted to change the young nigga's heart, quick fast and in a hurry.

Checkmate, who had been at home, laughed hysterically and couldn't believe that they had done that. Jania and Karbonado had really become close, and she honestly looked at him as a father figure.

*****

Saturday, Jania had been looking forward to seeing her friends so much that she had gotten very little sleep and was up at the crack of dawn. Checkmate decided that they would show up a little early to do some shopping. Karbonado went into The Finish Line and let the girls do their girl thing. While he was checking out a pair of Air Force Ones, three young teenagers approached him.

"Excuse me. Ain't you that guy that was all over the news a while back?" one of them asked. The three boys had been excitedly whispering before they had gone up to him.

"Nah, lil homie, I don't know what you talkin' about," Karbonado replied.

"Oh, my bad," he said and they all walked off.

Karbonado started checking out different shoes again, and two minutes later, the same teenagers approached him, one with a .357 out. "Say, look out!" the boy shouted.

When Karbonado turned around, he had no time to react before the four shots rang out.

"Young Hogg say what's up!" he shouted, shot at Karbonado once more, then the three teens took off running out of the mall, leaving Karbonado to die.

*****

Checkmate and Jania were in Victoria's Secret shopping when they heard the gunshots. They didn't know where the shots came from, but the way everybody was screaming and running out of The Finish Line, Checkmate began to worry. She pulled out her phone and called Karbonado. After calling five times, she walked over there.

"Let's go, Nia. We need to find Karbonado. We can come back later." She grabbed the girl's hand and rushed out Victoria's Secret and walked quickly towards The Finish Line.

Once they made it to the other store, she noticed people standing around someone. When she got closer, she could not believe it was Karbonado. "Noooo!" she screamed.

She got on the floor and grabbed him and rocked him back and forth in her arms as she cried. Jania stood there and cried as well. She didn't know what to do.

After what seemed like hours, the paramedics finally showed up. They had to wrestle Checkmate to get her to let him go so they could work on him. Once she was out of the way and they began to care for him, a paramedic announced, "We have a pulse!"

Jania finally pulled out of her trance and called Rowdy.

"What's up, Jania?" Rowdy asked, happy to hear from the girl she considered her niece.

"Rowdy, Karbonado got shot!"

Jania could hear the panic in Rowdy's voice. "What! Where is he and where is Checkmate?" She was hollering her questions into the phone.

"We are all in the mall. Me and Checkmate were in Victoria's Secret, and he went to The Finish Line. That's where he was shot, and Checkmate is going crazy. She won't let the paramedics do their job!"

"Jania, I'm on my way. I'll be there in 15 minutes." By the time Jania hung up, the police had gotten there and pulled Checkmate to the side to calm her down.

CHAPTER 12

$$$

Young Hogg was at the house playing with his niece. Ever since her dad got killed, he would call Ashley daily and make sure she was okay. It hurt him when Ashley would tell him how Kenya would cry and ask for her father every night. Young Hogg decided that maybe it would be good to have her around him, that way he could at least try to fill the void.

While he was playing with Kenya, he got a phone call. "Yo, what's up?"

"Say, Hogg, I got some good news!" Dewayne shouted.

"What's up, Wayne?" Young Hogg asked.

"My youngins just fired Karbonado's ass up!"

"Oh, yeah. Where did they catch him slippin'?" Young Hogg couldn't believe that maybe, just maybe, his brother's and sister's lives had been avenged.

"The nigga was in The Finish Line at Deerbrook Mall. Youngin walked right up to him and popped his top!"

"What?!" Young Hogg Asked. "They shot him in the mall?" Hogg hoped to hell he was playing.

"Hell yeah. I told my youngin if they ever ran into him or his people then give him the bizness on sight, and that's what they did." Dewayne bragged as if he had popped Karbonado.

"Damn! Damn! Damn! Do you not know that it's cameras all over that fuckin' mall? Fuck! You stupid son of a bitch! Y'all gonna get everybody locked up!" Young Hogg was pissed, knowing that this might bring down some serious heat on him.

"Calm down, Hogg, and let me check things out. But let's just look at it like this: We got him and now we need to get that bitch 'cause she is a fuckin' pain in the ass."

"Yeah, a'ight. You just better make sure yo' goons keep their mouths shut if they get popped. 'Cause if anything come back to me, I'ma hold you responsible." Young Hogg wasn't doin' no playing about warning him. And Dewayne knew he meant every word he said.

*****

Rowdy, Lil Moma and Checkmate were at the hospital waiting to find out about Karbonado. Rowdy tried to keep everyone calm, but that wasn't an easy task. Checkmate was quiet and it seemed like her whole mind had gone blank. She sat in the chair with Karbonado's blood still on her hands and clothes.

While they were waiting, about 20 members of the cartel showed up to see about Karbonado. It was so many people there, the security officers had to ask them to leave. They all looked to Rowdy, and after she ordered them out, they agreed to leave and meet her when she called them. The doctor couldn't believe all of the visitors were for one person. She had been working at the hospital for more than ten years and had never seen anything close to that crowd. "This man must be someone famous," she told herself.

About five minutes later, Dr. Conner came into the waiting room. "Who's here for Mr. Jason Lewis, Jr.." she questioned.

"We are," Rowdy answered.

"Can you all come with me down the hall, please?" When they had a little more privacy, Dr. Conner explained that Karbonado's surgery had gone well, but that because he had lost so much blood, he was in a coma.

Lil Moma and Checkmate broke down even more. Jania also took the doctor's report very hard. Even though Karbonado had been a complete asshole the first time she met him, they had become very close. Many nights they would sit up and listen to music and she would share her plans about her dream to be a rapper. He even promised that he would get a studio built for her. That had just been last week, but now he was damn near dead and she couldn't tell him that she loved him.

Checkmate finally spoke up. "So will he come out of his coma?" she asked. "And if so, how long will it take?"

"Well," the doctor said, "he could wake up anytime. It could be now or it could be six months." She paused, looking at them with concern. "He could never wake up again. But we aren't going to talk like that. We are going to think positive. I believe in God, and I know God will deliver him. Maybe not as soon as we want, but He will deliver him."

After explaining everything else to them, Dr. Conner advised them to go home and get some rest and come back the following day. She promised that she would make sure they got to visit Karbonado. Rowdy and Lil Moma agreed, but Checkmate and Jania weren't trying to hear it.

"Excuse me," Dr. Conner said, "let me talk to her for a minute." The others walked a few feet away, leaving Checkmate with the doctor.

Dr. Conner grabbed Checkmate by the hand and spoke to her in a motherly fashion. "Look, baby, I know what it's like to love someone then lose them. I know how you feel, but, baby, Jason will be alright. You don't have anything to worry about. I will do everything in my power to make sure he's okay in here. And I promise you'll see him tomorrow. Just go home and clean yourself up. Do you think he would want you to sit around in those filthy clothes?" With her last words, Dr. Conner playfully hugged Checkmate.

Checkmate chuckled a little. "He better want me around no matter how I look. I don't care if my clothes was smothered in dooky."

They both shared a laugh at Checkmate's joke. But she had to admit that the doctor was right. Her man always loved to be around a clean bitch that was smelling good. "You right, Dr. Conner. I will go home, shower, and get some rest. But you better make sure my man is taken care of. I'm serious."

Dr. Conner nodded her head to let Checkmate know that she understood.

*****

Kaci had just finished watching the news. She couldn't believe that someone had the balls to shoot Karbonado in the mall. Kaci knew that most likely he had a price on his head because everybody knew that Deerbrook Mall had cameras everywhere. And everybody knew who Karbonado was.

While she was getting ready to take a bath, she got a phone call from her mother. "Hey, Momma."

"Hey, baby. I just wanted to tell you that we got Jason Lewis at our hospital. He's doing better, but he lost so much blood, and that caused him to slip into a coma."

90

This made Kaci sad because she really did like him as a person. He had a good heart and he was the one that helped boost her career. That was the main reason her mother, Dr. Conner, was going to make sure that she took care of him. She appreciated how he helped her daughter and her grandbaby.

"Momma, make sure he's okay in there. If any police try to talk to him, you tell them that they need to contact me first, then give them my number."

Kaci's mother accepted the instructions. "Okay, baby, I'll do everything I can," she promised.

After she finished talking to her mother, Kaci started praying. She could not afford for Karbonado to die because he was her meal ticket. Ever since she met him, her lifestyle had changed. She was able to buy whatever she wanted and do whatever she wanted. Last week, she had even bought a Bentley coupe.

"Damn, I feel sorry for whoever did that shit to him," she thought. She knew that they type of men Karbonado had on his side were not to be fucked with.

*****

After leaving the hospital, the ride home was very quiet. Each of the girls were in their own thoughts. Once they made it to Karbonado's house, Lil Moma and Rowdy decided to stay there. Checkmate went and took her bloody clothes off. After throwing them in a trash bag, she made herself some bath water and jumped in.

As she was relaxing in the tub, all she could think about was how she was gonna do the niggas that tried to kill Karbonado. There was no way she was gonna let anybody get away with that.

After she finished taking a bath, she got out of the tub and dried off. Then she walked to the bed and laid down. She couldn't stop crying because every time she looked around the room, all she saw was him. That would be the first time since making up that they hadn't slept in the bed together and that was the hardest thing she had to deal with. An hour later, she finally cried herself to sleep.

*****

The next morning, the twins got up early and were ready to go see Karbonado. Jania had just come downstairs and she was ready too. "Hey, Aunt Rowdy. Hey, Aunt Moma." She gave both of them hugs.

They hadn't seen Checkmate since she went to her room the previous night. They decided to all go together to see how she was doing. When the girls walked into the room, they couldn't hold back the laughter. Rowdy was laughing the hardest.

"Damn, Checkmate! Get yo' big booty ass up!" Rowdy slapped Checkmate on her ass.

Checkmate got up and wrestled Rowdy down. Lil Moma and Jania were laughing because Checkmate was still naked. She got on top of Rowdy and started talking shit.

"I'm up now, hoe. Get me up off you." It felt good to Checkmate to play and release a little tension.

Rowdy couldn't get her off, so Lil Moma jumped in and dove on top of Checkmate. "Get yo' naked ass off of my sister."

Before they knew it, all three of them were wrestling on the bed and laughing and having fun like they were kids again. "Y'all, come on, we got to hit the hospital," Lil Moma reminded them.

"Give me a minute to get myself together!" Checkmate hollered. "And damn, Nia, you gonna let them hoes jump me like that?" They all started laughing again.

When Checkmate finished getting ready, they all jumped in the car and went to the hospital. Upon arrival, they walked in and asked the clerk for Dr. Conner. They explained that they were Jason Lewis' family and that Dr. Conner had told them to ask for her specifically. The clerk called the doctor and was told that she would be down momentarily.

Dr. Conner arrived about two minutes later and smiled once she saw how Checkmate had cleaned herself up. She could still see the stress on the younger woman's face, however, and it was obvious that she had spent the night crying.

"How are y'all doing?" she asked. The girls just nodded, and Dr. Conner said, "Come this way. I know you are ready to see Mr. Lewis." She knew they weren't really interested in small talk; they only wanted to know how the man they all loved was doing.

Upon entering the room, they were all devastated. Each of them began crying. Dr. Conner hated to see them in such pain, and after all her years as a doctor, she had seen this too many times.

Checkmate remembered that the doctor said Karbonado might be able to hear even though he was not responding. So she made a promise to him. "Baby, I'm gonna get those niggas. They tried to knock you off, but I'ma show 'em how it's done. And this time everybody get it, including kids. Everybody." Trembling in anger, Checkmate kissed his cheek, then walked out of the room. She was about to show the world the definition of a killer.

CHAPTER 13

$$$

It had been three days since the attempt on Karbonado's life. The Black Diamond Cartel had been causing so much trouble the feds had to set up a 24-hour security detail inside the Garden City Projects.

Young Hogg was pissed because his money was now at a standstill. And to make matters worse, the three teens were now in custody, being charged with aggravated assault with a deadly weapon. All three of the boys were seventeen and had never been in trouble. Because of that, the judge gave each of them a $60,000 bond. The problem they now had was they had been trying to reach Dewayne and couldn't get an answer.

Young Hogg had already told Dewayne to go and bail them out, but for some reason, he had taken his time. After spending what felt like months in the county jail, all three of them had their names called for release.

"Damn, about time!" Dojo shouted.

They all rushed to the desk to fill out all of the paperwork. Two hours later, they were finally walking out of the jail. Outside the jail, they decided to wait on Dewayne. They figured he would be out there somewhere waiting on them. After 10 minutes, a black van pulled up and six men jumped out with AK47s and jammed them in the boys' faces. They grabbed the boys, shoved them into the van, and pulled off.

In minutes, the teens were tied up and scared to death.

"Why y'all tie us up?" Jojo asked. "Where y'all taking us?"

No one answered him and they began to freak out. "Look, whatever it is, you can call my cousin, Dewayne. If it's money, he got it and will pay you!" Dojo tried to bribe the people behind the darkness but still got no response.

Whatever it was they knew, these guys were not trying to reveal anything.

They rode in the van in absolute silence before they came to a stop. The six men pulled the boys out of the van and took them inside a white warehouse. Three women stood inside the door, obviously waiting for them.

"I'm glad you boys could make it," Rowdy said, a nasty smile on her face.

Finally, one of the other boys spoke up. "Man, what the fuck you bitches thinkin', got these niggas pullin' guns out on us and all this." Before he knew what was happening, he screamed. Checkmate had stabbed him in the shoulder blade.

"First off, motherfucka, you gonna watch yo' mouth. Second, you only speak when I ask a question!" She stabbed him in the left leg to make her point.

"Ahhh! Damn! Why you doin' this to me? What I do to you?" The boy was screaming and had tears rolling down his dark brown cheeks.

Checkmate took the butt of her 9mm and slammed it across his nose. "Didn't I tell you not to speak unless I ask you a question? Matter fact, I'm done talkin' to you."

Boom! Boom! Boom! Boom!

She shot him four times in the face. "Now, who else wanna speak without permission?!" She screamed, barely controlling her anger. Dojo and the other boy wouldn't say a word. His friend even pissed on himself. "Listen, and you better take my advice," she said, pointing at the dead body. "I'm only gonna ask one time. If I feel you trying to bullshit me, you know what it is." She pointed at the dead body again. "That's how I'ma leave yo' ass."

She stared at each boy to make sure they understood her warning before she asked her question. Now, which one of y'all shot Karbonado?"

Without hesitation, as if they were Siamese twins joined at the brain, they both pointed at the boy with his face missing.

"Okay," Checkmate continued, "Who the fuck ordered you to do that shit?"

Jojo answered her, his voice shaking like a kid going through puberty. "It was Dewayne. He told us that if we seen anybody from the Black Diamond Cartel, then shoot them on sight. He told us that Young Hogg had a half a mill for anybody that kill Karbonado. And the same for the female they call Checkmate."

She was pissed that Young Hogg continued to try her gangster. But he was about to see how she played the game of murder. "Where Dewayne live?" she asked. The two boys gave her the address, and Checkmate sent her goons to go and pick Dewayne and anybody with him up.

* * * * *

While Checkmate and the twins were at the warehouse waiting on their goons to come back with Dewayne, Jania was at the hospital with

Karbonado. Whenever the twins or Checkmate weren't in the streets putting in work, they were there sitting with him also.

Checkmate had told Jania to talk to him even though he could not talk back. She poured her heart out to him as she sat and held his hand. "Karbonado, I miss you so much. It's crazy how at first you didn't like me!" Jania laughed to herself. "But I want you to know that I love you. I can't lie. A lot of times I think of you as my father. I mean I never had one around, but every day I spent around you, I felt like daddy's little girl.

"I never told you these things because I didn't want you to decide to kick me out of the house again. But, you know, I will never forget the things you taught me. I still write music, but it's not the same without you. I mean, who else do I turn to and ask for advice when it comes to certain parts of my songs?"

While Jania was talking, she was interrupted. "Excuse me. Do you mind giving me a few minutes to change his bandage?" The nurse had spoken, but Dr. Conner had come in with her to examine Karbonado and see how he was progressing.

Jania shook her head. "Sure. I don't mind anything that is going to help him."

"Baby, how old are you and who are you to Mr. Lewis?" Dr. Conner questioned.

"I'm sixteen and Mr. Lewis is my father," Jania answered. It was only a small lie. Blood alone didn't make someone family, and sperm alone didn't make someone a father.

"Oh, okay. I was only asking because I noticed that you have been here daily. I could tell that you are close to him."

"Yeah, we always had sit downs and just talked about whatever, no matter what it was," Jania expressed.

Dr. Conner smiled. "I understand that feeling well, baby." She finished his examination, noting there was little change, and the nurse finished changing his bandage. They both left the room together.

*****

After waiting nearly three hours, the goons finally showed up with Dewayne, his baby, and the baby's mother. Dewayne knew his life was over when he saw the body that belonged to his kin folk. All he could do is beg for the lives of his family.

"Listen, y'all wanna kill me, then I accept that. But leave them out of it. They have nothin' to do with me and my decisions." He wasn't too proud to beg.

"You tried to kill Karbonado, and you would've tried to kill me too. By the way, my name Checkmate." She stuck her hand out for him to shake it. His eyes widened upon hearing her name. He knew that she didn't play games, and he was suddenly hating himself for even trying to collect the money Young Hogg had put on their heads.

"Listen," she told him, "I'll make you a deal of a lifetime."

"And what's that?" he asked.

"Give me Young Hogg. I want to know where he's hidin'. If you tell me, I'll let yo' girl and yo' son live. But you will still die at my hands. What do you say?"

He put his head down 'cause he knew he was fucked. He didn't know where Young Hogg rested his head. "Honestly, I don't know," he admitted, knowing it meant his death and the death of his family.

Boom!

Checkmate shot and killed his son. Dewayne's baby mama was now screaming.

Boom! Boom! Boom!

Checkmate shot and killed her too. Then she looked him in the eyes and kissed him on the cheek. "This," she said, "is the kiss of death."

She shot him in the throat then shot and killed the other two boys.

*****

At 7:00 that night, everybody in Garden City was outside. The police had kept their presence known full-time to make sure people weren't out in the streets killing one another. The Garden City Cartel had already been ordered to stop all transactions by Young Hogg. That meant no dope deals and no murder. The last few days had been drama free.

That's until a white Denali pulled up with tinted windows.

For a moment, some people were worried, but then they remembered that it was no way the Denali would make it past the cops if they started a war. After a few seconds, the passenger door opened and a man stepped out. He opened the back door of the truck and pulled out two duffle bags, walked over to one of Young Hogg's soldiers and delivered a message. "This here is some money for Young Hogg. Make sure he gets every dime that's in here. Tell him it's a note in the pocket on the side of the bag." The man stopped talking, then walked away and got back in the truck.

Once the truck pulled away, the young soulja carried the bags inside the apartment and called Young Hogg.

"Yo' what's up?" Hogg answered the phone.

"Say, I just received two duffle bags from some guy. He said for me to make sure you got every dime."

"Mike, how much did he leave? It wasn't nobody supposed to drop you no money." Young Hogg was confused by the drop off.

Mike was now confused also. "Well, he left a note. Do you want me to open it and read the note to you?"

"Yeah, read it to me," Hogg directed him.

Mike opened the letter and read it out loud. "Young Hogg, I see you still haven't learned 'bout fuckin' with us. I told you the next time I make a hit, I wasn't gonna let nobody make it. You touched the wrong boss, but guess what? You missed. I also heard 'bout the money you put on me and Karbonado head. Well, here's two duffle bags of yo' money back. Consider it a refund, bitch nigga!"

"Mike, open them duffle bags and see what's up." Young Hogg was definitely worried about what Checkmate had done now.

Mike opened one of the bags and couldn't believe what he was seeing. "Ohh, shit!" he yelled. "Damn, that's nasty!"

"What's up, Mike?" Young Hogg asked, nearly panicking.

"These motherfuckas got cut off heads in them! Hogg, man, it's Dewayne, his baby mama, his son, and two of those young niggas that tried to kill Karbonado. It's just their heads wrapped in plastic.

"Damn, these motherfuckas brought this shit over here, knowing the cops been posted up out here."

Young Hogg was now pissed. He couldn't believe Checkmate would go that far. He now knew that he had to do everything he could to get her and Karbonado off the streets of Houston. He also decided that his wife and kids were no longer safe.

CHAPTER 14

$$$

"**D**amn, this shit crazy," Checkmate said to herself. She had just taken a home pregnancy test and it was positive. Karbonado had been in a coma for a month and a half with no signs of waking up, and here she was pregnant with his child.

Checkmate had been up there everyday to see him. No matter what, she always made it to his beside. She would show up and climb into his bed and just talk to him. A lot of times she would do everything the nurses would allow her to, believing it was the only way she could take care of her man. She would bathe him, rub his skin down with lotion, then clip his nails. She would also keep his mouth and teeth clean with the swabs and solution the nurses brought in.

One day, while she was pouring her heart out to him, two detectives came in and interrupted her conversation. "Excuse us, ma'am. I'm Detective Moore and this is Detective Carter. Do you mind if we ask a couple of questions?"

Checkmate stared long and hard at the female detective before she answered. "Yeah, what do y'all need?"

"First, let me ask who you are to Mr. Lewis?" Detective Moore questioned.

"He's my fiancé," Checkmate claimed.

"Oh, okay. Well, we wanted to know if you had any idea why those three young men shot Mr. Lewis. I mean, you were at the mall with him, right?"

"Yes," Checkmate answered. "We went to the mall together, but we split up when I wanted to go inside of Victoria's Secrets. You know how men are about being seen in a woman's store." They both smiled.

Even Detective Moore had to admit she was right. Whenever the detective tried to get her husband to go into certain stores, he also refused. "Yeah, I agree and understand that. Well do you know why those men would want to try and kill Mr. Lewis?"

"No, I do not," Checkmate said, her response dry.

"The three men who shot Mr. Lewis were found dead the day after they bonded out of jail. Someone delivered their heads to the Garden City Projects. Have you heard anything about that?"

"Detective Moore, I believe I answered the questions you asked me to answer. Now, will you two please allow me to spend time with my fiancé in peace?"

Again, the two women stood staring at each other, both understanding that this meeting was going nowhere. But Detective Moore didn't want to give up so easily. "Excuse me, but you could at least answer the last question. Unless you're guilty of knowing something?"

"No," Checkmate said, finally showing a little temper, "I will not answer anymore questions. You asked if you could ask me a couple of questions, and unfortunately for you, you asked two in one sentence.

Still, I let that slide as one question. Then you asked again and I answered. Now you askin' a third question. If you want anymore answers, contact my lawyer, Kaci Conner. I believe you both know who that is." Checkmate smiled as she looked at Detective Carter, who had chosen to remain quiet until now.

He looked at his partner then told Checkmate, "You have a nice day, miss...?" He was fishing.

"Mrs. Lewis," Checkmate replied with a tight smile on her face.

Detective Carter frowned, unable to cover his anger at the fact that she wasn't an easy target to peal for information. Both detectives just walked out of the room, leaving Checkmate smiling that mean smile of hers.

That had been over a week ago, and now here she was standing in her bathroom looking at a pregnancy test. "I got to up my security," she told herself. "I can't allow myself to be an easy target. "

And that's what she did. Everywhere she went, she now had two shooters in the car with her and two more in a truck that followed her around 24 hours a day. She broke it down into three shifts: 6-2, 2-10, and 10-6. Each shift had six shooters that were being paid $7,000 each per week. She had no problem spending $126,000 a week to make sure her house was safe, and Jania did not leave her sight.

Checkmate advised the twins to do the same, and they agreed. Now they had twelve gunmen on their property at all times, and those men were loving the money they were making. It was no way somebody was going to make it onto the property and not find themselves waking up in a body bag.

*****

It had been a week since Checkmate found out that she was pregnant. She still hadn't told Rowdy, Lil Moma, or Jania. She didn't want to share that information with anyone until Karbonado heard it from her first.

She got up that morning and went to see him. When she walked into his room, Dr. Conner was there, making sure everything was okay with him. Checkmate and Kaci's mom had built a lil bond. They would sit and talk, both enjoying the conversations they had.

"Hey, Dr. Conner," Checkmate said, a genuine smile on her face.

"Hey, baby, how you doing?"

They talked for a few minutes then Dr. Conner left to allow Checkmate some time alone with Karbonado. She took off her shoes and climbed in the bed beside him. Once she was comfortable, she began talking to him. "Hey, baby. I bet you been wondering where I been, huh? Well, the reason I wasn't here earlier this morning is because I was sick. I thought it was because I been runnin' the streets non-stop, but last week I found out I am pregnant. You know what that mean, right? That mean you need to get yo' ass up, 'cause I ain't takin' care of this baby by myself." Checkmate giggled. "Anyway, I miss you so much. And you was right. Our first time became special because every time I think about those moments, I laugh at how you ended up in the emergency room."

Her eyes became a little teary. "Baby, I hope you up when I give birth to our child. I know he or she gonna be spoiled as hell! Oh yeah, I boosted our security around the house. I just felt it would be good for us and our baby to be guarded heavy. Our whole squad is doin' good. Everybody is on money. But the thing is, we are almost out of work and I don't know what to do on that part. I don't know the plug and I don't want to go score from somebody else and create bad blood. But I'll try to figure something out.

104

"Oh, and your girl been doin' good in school. That's the only time she's not with me or the twins, 'cause I'm keeping a close eye on her. But she call herself havin' a crush on some boy named Trigga." Checkmated laughed about this. "He's 17 and the brother of one of my workers. I haven't really seen anything wrong with him, but she told him that she wouldn't even consider dating until after he met her daddy. Can you believe this girl using the daddy card again?

"I can't lie though. She been here to see you everyday. Honestly, I get jealous because she would ask me to leave the room while she talk to you. And a lot of times, I wonder what she talk about. It's not that I don't trust her. I just be wantin' to know what it is. But I respect her wish because she always give me that same space when I come to talk to you."

Checkmate spent a few hours talking to Karbonado, then she gave him a kiss and left to meet Rowdy and Lil Moma. She also had to pick Jania up from school.

*****

"I think that girl know something," Detective Moore said.

"Yeah, I feel the same way," Detective Carter responded.

"I noticed when you mentioned the three men being killed that she ended the conversation."

"I have an idea. Maybe we could get the judge to sign off on us placing a bug in his room."

Detective Carter liked her suggestion. "Yeah, we could try that, but what if we can't get the judge to approve it?"

"I don't know what we'll do, but we have to at least play that card first. Who knows, we might get lucky." Detective Moore smiled at the possibilities.

"Alright, but meanwhile, I'm going to do a background check on this Ashley Simone. I believe she knows something about those young boys being murdered."

That settled, Detective Moore decided it was time for lunch, and Detective Carter began looking into Ashley Simone's background.

Moore made it to her car, heading to Chili's. She loved going there to eat, but most of the time she just wanted some alone time to reflect on her personal issues.

She was a 33-year-old woman with no kids, who had just found her way clear of an abusive relationship. Her sisters did not comprehend how she was a cop being abused.

The oldest of five, Toya Moore was of mixed descent. Her mother was Black, and her father was both Black and Mexican. She was five foot six and thick in all the right places.

Moore sat down and ordered her food. As she looked around, people watching as any good detective did, she observed a couple walk in, holding hands and smiling. Once she got a good look, she couldn't believe it was Kiara. Kiara appeared to be very happy, but what bothered Moore was the guy Kiara was with.

Detective Moore had been a cop for over eight years, and if there was one thing she had learned, it was how to read people. She knew without a doubt that they guy Kiara was with was a drug dealer. "Nigga got on a Frank Mueller watch with diamonds, and Cartier frames with a Gucci outfit. Yeah, I know he ain't gettin' it working a nine to five."

She watched the couple sit in a booth close to the restrooms. Although her food had come, she suddenly wasn't very hungry anymore. She was more interested in what Kiara was doing. She waited until their food arrived, then she got up to go to the restroom, pretending to be surprised to see Kiara of her way.

Kiara looked at her and for a second she wanted to pretend to not know her. Instead, she asked, "Toya, how are you, and what are you doing in here at this time of day?" Kiara tried to not let her nervousness show, because she still hadn't told Damn Fool that she was a cop.

"I just stopped by to grab something to eat and just so happened to see you on my way to the restroom," Detective Moore lied.

Oh, okay. I'm just spending a lil time with my friend." Kiara smiled as if it wasn't a big deal.

Detective Moore asked, "Well, aren't you going to introduce me to your friend?"

Kiara looked at Damn Fool then back at Moore. "Kevin, this is Toya, another friend. Toya, this is Kevin."

"Hi, I'm glad to meet you." Detective Moore shook his hand.

She didn't stay at their table long, wanting to play it cool and let them finish enjoying their meal together.

"So where do you know her from?" Damn Fool asked Kiara.

"She's from my neighborhood," she replied.

"Oh, okay. It seem like you became frustrated once she came around." He had noticed a little tension between the two women.

"I just hate it when we're spending time together and someone interrupts our moment." Kiara held her breath, hoping he would believe the partial truth.

He laughed. "I want you to do your best tomorrow. I know you have been a little down because of the situation with your friend. But allow God to work in your life along with your friend's life." She was really trying to encourage him.

"Yeah, I'm gonna give it my best shot. You made a way for me to make some legal bread, so I'm gonna see how this turns out."

Damn Fool was really feeling Kiara. He loved how she didn't judge him and how she was willing to help him. Most women he had met were all about his money. But Kiara wasn't that type of person and she showed it everyday.

Kiara was feeling Damn Fool as well. They had been talking almost two months, and he had never came at her about sex. She also liked how he was willing to give up the lifestyle he was used to living if the comedy thing worked out. No one else in his life would have ever considered the fact that Damn Fool would even consider doing something legal if given the opportunity. But Kiara saw something in him that he didn't even see in himself.

*****

Jania was standing outside of Nimitz High School on her phone. She had been talking to Trigga everyday since they met. Trigga was an eleventh grader at Westfield High School and had the skills to become an NBA star. He had already gotten several scholarship offers from colleges like Duke, North Carolina, Texas, and UCLA.

Trigga met Jania one day at Nimitz's homecoming game against Aldine High. "Look out, baby girl, let ya boy rap to you for a minute," he said with a smile on his face.

Jania stopped and turned to face the boy that had grabbed her arm. "Why are you putting your filthy hands on me?" she said with an attitude.

"Damn, lil mama, I just wanna rap to you for a minute." She noticed the smile never left his face. A lot of boys would have gotten mad about her attitude.

"Listen, young doc," she said sarcastically, "I don't like rap, so please beat ya feet and keep your hands to yourself." He just kept staring at her with that goofy smile. "You don't know who I am?" she asked.

"No, that's the problem. I'm tryna get to know you and you trippin'."

She couldn't help but laugh. Most niggas would have backed off, but he wouldn't. She figured she would try one more time. "Does the name Karbonado ring a bell in your head?" she asked.

When she said the name, she saw his facial expression change. "Yeah, I heard of that name, but what that got to do with anything?"

"That's my father," she said with pride.

"Damn." He said this softly as he put his head down. "Do you know somebody name Troy, but they call him T-Rich?" he asked.

"Yeah, I've heard the name, but I'm not sure where."

"Well, that's my brother, and he work for some female under Karbonado name Checkmate."

When she heard Checkmate's name, Jania really smiled. "That's my mother." It was an innocent lie, if not the truth, since Checkmate took her in.

Ever since that day, they had become cool with each other.

While Jania was talking to Trigga, Checkmate finally pulled up in her grey Range Rover. "Trigga, I'm about to get in the car, so I'll talk to you later on when I get to the house." Jania hung up the phone and got in.

"What's up, Nia? How was school?"

"It was good until I had to knock some sense in this girl."

Checkmate could only chuckle. She had already rubbed off on Jania, and she knew it. She always told the girl not to take no shit from them girls, and that's what Jania refused to do. "Have you gone to visit Karbonado today?" Jania questioned.

"Yeah, I went to see his stubborn ass. That nigga just won't get up!" Checkmate was very frustrated by the continued coma. Jania didn't say anything else. Checkmate sighed and said, "Nia, guess what?" She was excited to finally tell someone.

"What's up?"

"I'm pregnant."

"What?!" Jania asked, suddenly excited herself. "So I'm about to have a lil brother or sister?"

"Yep, I'm pregnant. I just hope this nigga wake his ass up. I wouldn't want him to miss out on his firstborn." Checkmate had tears running down her cheeks.

"Do Aunt Rowdy and Lil Moma know?"

"No. I plan on tellin' them in a minute. I didn't want to tell nobody until I told Karbonado first."

Jania understood and didn't ask any more questions. She turned the music up and began to text Trigga.

The 20-minute ride home was quiet. Checkmate dropped Jania off at their house then went over to Rowdy's house. When she got there, Rowdy was playing Pac-Man with Lil Moma.

"What's up, Checkmate?" Rowdy shouted.

"Hey, y'all, what's up?" Checkmate hugged both of them. Rowdy saw the smile on her face, and said, "Girl, what you smiling so hard for, 'cause my brother gave you some on Viagra again?" All three of them had a laughing fit.

"No, but that Viagra caused him to plant a seed in me!" she shouted, excitedly.

"So you telling us we about to have a niece or nephew?" the twins asked.

"That's exactly what I'm sayin'. I found out last week." Checkmate kind of looked down during this confession.

"Last week?!" both girls yelled. "So why in the hell is we just findin' out?" Neither of them was really upset, they were just wondering.

"Because I wanted to share that moment with yo' brother first. I went and told him, and now I'm tellin' my girls."

"Okay, so that mean we need tear up the mall. I'm goin' to get the baby some fly shit!" Rowdy was serious about shopping for her niece or nephew.

"Girl, we don't even know what she havin," Lil Moma said. "You always tryin' to find a reason to tear somebody store up."

Checkmate said, "Bitch think she slick. Don't be tryna use my baby as an excuse to go on one of your $20,000 shopping sprees."

"Whatever. Y'all wasn't sayin' shit when I bought Christian Louboutin shoes!" she bragged.

"That's because we knew you only bought them for us so we couldn't put up much fuss about you buying a beach," Checkmate told her.

"Rowdy, you gotta serious shoppin' addiciton," Lil Moma told her. "You got a four bedroom home with no husband or kids, and every room got a closet full of shit you ain't gonna wear."

Rowdy couldn't deny it. She knew she went overboard when it was time to shop. "Y'all right. I do got too much shit," she admitted.

"Hey," Checkmate said, changing the subject, "y'all know Damn Fool doin' standup comedy now?" The twins were surprised to hear it. She continued, "Yeah, Kaci Conner friend got him on the set to open up for Mike Epps tomorrow!"

"I can't believe that shit," Rowdy admitted. "Karbonado would have loved to watch his boy tell jokes."

"Yeah, that nigga funny as hell, even when he not tryin'," Lil Moma said.

"Well we need to go support him, 'cause I'm down for anybody that want to make something of their self," Rowdy said, and Checkmate and Lil Moma agreed. "But I'ma say this: If I waste my money on some corny jokes, I'm kickin' his ass for embarrassin' himself!"

CHAPTER 15

$$$

"I hope this nigga funny like you say, 'cause you know I don't like wastin' money," Kaci said to Kiara.

"Girl, shut up, 'cause you ain't spent a dime to get in here, unless you talking about that five dollar drink yo' cheap ass bought!"

Kiara laughed. "Shit, I may have spent five dollars, but guess what? This drink gonna do the same thing that expensive shit you paid for gonna do." Kaci wasn't cheap, but alcohol was alcohol.

"Look," Kiara said, pointing at the twins, Checkmate, and Jania, "there go them gangstas."

Kaci just shook her head. "Girl, what's up with you? Why you always start trippin' whenever you see them?"

"It's nothing really. You know how I feel about criminals."

Kaci looked at her, astonished by her hypocrisy. "Um, hello, Damn Fool is a criminal!" she reminded Kiara.

"Yeah, but I'm trying to change that."

"Listen, Kiara, you can't change a street nigga. You might be able to slow him down. But you are not gonna change him!"

Kiara raised her eyebrows as she said, "We will see."

By the time they finished debating, Damn Fool was making his way to the stage. Kiara and Kaci didn't notice at first, but suddenly they realized that the club had at least 50 members from the Black Diamond Cartel. They were all cheering and supporting Damn Fool.

"Y'all calm down!" Damn Fool said. "Calm dawn! I ain't even start tellin' jokes and y'all cheerin'." They all laughed. "Damn, it's too many Black people in here! Yeah, that's one strike against us. Y'all get ready, the police will be at the front door any minute." Everybody laughed, even though there was some truth in the joke.

"Excuse me, Black people. We received a call sayin' y'all were disturbin' the peace, the officer said. And y'all know when you hear the words 'disturbing the peace', just turn around and put yo' hands behind ya back, 'cause you goin' to jail!" So far, the crowd was feeling him. "I'm just gonna be real, I hate fuckin' cops! Yeah, I know it's some undercovers in here, that's why I'm expressing my feelings. You see this stage, this stage is considered private property, which means you can't come up here and fuck with me. So put ya handcuffs back on ya waist 'cause you ain't using them tonight!"

After a 20-minute set, Damn Fool had the club laughing out of control. Mike Epps came and did his best comedy too, and everybody felt like they got their money's worth.

When the show was over they left and went to Damn Fool house Kiara was happy to spend some time with Damn Fool. "I'm proud of you. I told you that you were funny."

"I can't lie, I didn't feel those first few jokes was funny. But after I got in that zone, it was a wrap."

Kiara smiled. A little bragging never hurt anybody. "So how is your friend Karbonado?"

"I don't know. I plan to go see him tomorrow. It's hard seein' my nigga like that though," he admitted.

"Yeah, I understand. How do you think he will feel about you getting out of the game?"

Damn Fool looked at her for a few seconds without speaking. "What do you mean 'how would he feel'? That's been my nigga since we were kids. His dad took me in when I had nobody else. If I decide to leave the game, my nigga will be cool with it." His voice left no doubt that he was aggravated.

"Look, don't get mad at me because I give a damn about you! I want to see you make something of yourself, not become somebody's slave in prison!" The moment she let those words out, she regretted them.

"Slave?" Damn Fool questioned. "Fuck you talkin' about? You been to college and got all these degrees and I bet you don't own shit! You live in a bullshit one bedroom. Me, I got a five bedroom in Summerwood. You drive a bullshit Altima, and I drive a Range Rover and a S55D. And I do what I want, whenever I want. It might be illegal, but at least I'm not stressed out about no bills. Now if you can't accept me for who I am, then move around!" He waited on her response.

"You right about everything you said. I don't own shit, and I already knew you were a drug dealer the day we met and I still entertained the thought of maybe changing you. That's my fault and you have the right to be upset." Kiara had tears in her eyes now. "Kevin, I really like you. I know it's only been a few months, but I honestly have grown to have strong feelings for you. I haven't been happy in so long and whenever I'm with you, I'm at peace. It may seem crazy to you, but I'm not trying to lose you."

"Kiara, I care about you too, but I'ma be 100 with you. I don't have plans to leave the streets right now. I got so much I want to accomplish with this tax-free money." He laughed. "But I can tell you this: my team is not to be fucked with. Plus, we got the baddest lawyer in the state on our team. So stop worrying about what I do in the streets, and let's focus on what I do in yo' sheets."

He kissed her then and she kissed him back. Damn Fool began to undress her. He laid her on the bed and made love to her with his tongue.

"Ooh, baby, I'm cumin'!" Kiara screamed as her body trembled. "Damn, nigga, I see why they call you Damn Fool!" She moaned and squirmed on the bed until he stopped for a moment. They both burst out laughing.

"Damn, girl, you crazy."

Damn Fool brought his head up from between her legs and was about to kiss her, but she stopped him. "Uh, uh, Kevin, you was just lickin' some kat," she said laughing.

"Oh, yeah," Damn Fool said. He stuck his tongue out and started licking on her face and lips.

"Oooh, stop, boy! You nasty!" She tried to move away from his tongue. "Okay, okay, I'm sorry," Kiara screamed.

"Give me a kiss!" he yelled right back.

Kiara gave him a kiss and they started where they left off.

*****

The next morning, Damn Fool woke up with his dick in Kiara's mouth. She was sucking him so good that he started stuttering. "Da-da damn, baby, shi-shit!" he yelled, releasing his load down her throat. When he was finished, she got up and went to brush her teeth then got back in the bed.

"Damn, what did I do to deserve that mornin' treatment?" he asked, smiling.

"You put in some work, made a bitch almost have a heart attack with them orgasms," she said with a straight face.

"Shit, you put in some work, too. We fucked 12 times!"

He tried to kiss her, but she pulled away. "Uh, uh. Go brush your teeth first."

"That's cold," Damn Fool said, but got up and did what she said.

When he got back, he tried to get him some pussy, but she wasn't having it. "That's why I sucked you up. I thought it would drain you, but you still trying to get some!"

"Girl, I ain't tryna hear that." He gently pushed her legs open and entered her juice box.

"Oooh, baby, go easy on me. I'm still sore." She still moaned in pleasure. He pulled out of her and told her to turn over. She got on all fours and he began to punish her. "Damn, bae, oooh shit. Ahh, shit, baby. Fuck this pussy." She cried out over and over in ecstasy.

"Who this pussy belong to?" he asked, still pounding her pussy.

"Yours, baby, this pussy is yours!" she hollered. "Ooooh, I'm cummin! I'm cummin! Ahh!" She was screaming loud enough to wake up the dead as he pushed deep inside her and released his load.

"Damn, baby, you got good pussy!" he told her after he fell out, exhausted.

He laid down on his back and she laid her head on his chest. For the next ten minutes, they just laid there, not saying a word. Finally, Kiara confessed, "Baby, I love you."

"I love you too. But listen, I need you to stop worryin' so much and just be down with me. I'ma take care of you and treat you like you want to be treated, but you gotta love me for who I am and accept that I'm a street nigga."

"I will accept you for who you are. You did have a point earlier. I've been to school and always have done the right thing, and I don't own shit. Baby, I look at my friend, Kaci, and she's damn near became a millionaire overnight. And I honestly am jealous of her sometimes. I love my friend and I am happy for her, but I do want more than one bedroom." This confession hurt her in some ways. She didn't really want to admit she was just like most people.

"What do you want to do?" he asked.

"I want to do real estate. I got my license two years ago. I always dreamed of owning a lot of real estate, but what's a dream when you ain't got money?"

"I understand, and that's why my dream is to always have money 'cause money open up doors to get more money."

She laughed after thinking about what he said.

"Look, I'm gonna help you, but first thing you gotta do is let that bullshit job go. Then we about to open you an account. I got somebody with legal money that will give you a million dollars. You'll use that money to flip properties."

She was stunned and worried. "Are you sure nobody will be able to trace the money?"

"My friend owns a record label. You ever heard of Lil D?"

She nodded her head. "Yeah, Dawg House Records, right?"

"Yeah, well, he owe me a favor and I'll call him in on it."

She sighed. "Okay, I'm cool with all that. But I'm telling you, don't ever bring any drugs around me. And don't ever ask me to touch any drugs." The look on her face said she was serious.

"That's cool, but you know I blow weed daily," he said.

"I'm not talking about that," she assured. "I'm talking about the drugs for sale!"

"Okay, I got you!" he agreed.

They kissed then got up to hit the streets. Kiara was happy she could kick her job to the curb and couldn't wait until she was done. She got dressed, and she and Damn Fool left the apartment headed in two different directions.

CHAPTER 16

$$$

Checkmate was at the hospital visiting Karbonado when he began moving his eyes. She jumped up and ran to get Dr. Conner. When the doctor mad$$$e it to the room, Karbonado was wide awake. He just stared at Checkmate and Dr. Conner for what seemed like hours.

"Mr. Lewis, I know you can hear me. We are glad to have you back with us." As Dr. Conner began to examine him, she said, "Baby, give me a cup of water for him."

Checkmate brought the water and Dr. Conner helped him drink it. After he finished, he began talking. "What happened?" he asked.

"Baby, you was shot and went into a coma," Checkmate replied.

By this time, Rowdy, Lil Moma, and Jania came running into the room. "He's back, thank God!" Because they were all yelling, it was hard to tell who was saying what. The noise, however, was scaring Karbonado.

Completing her brief examination, Dr. Conner said, "He's going to be fine, but he has to learn how to walk all over again."

THE MURDER OF A BOSS

"That's small," Rowdy proclaimed, "I know my brother will be back up and running in no time."

Karbonado looked back and forth at his family. Dr. Conner knew he needed some time to gather his thoughts and she told the girls so.

"Damn, he been sleep for three months!" Rowdy wanted instant results.

"Baby, it's not the same kind of sleep. He needs to rest. Give him some time. He'll be ready to talk and start therapy soon.

The girls decided to allow him a rest break, Checkmate gave him a kiss before they all left. They were hungry and exited the hospital to go eat, at the conclusion of which Rowdy tried to force the group to go shopping for the baby.

"No!" Checkmate and Lil Moma yelled, and then Checkmate reminded her they didn't

even know the sex of the baby yet.

"Well, damn, y'all didn't have to yell at me," Rowdy said, pouting.

"We just know that if we go shoppin', you will go overboard," Lil Moma told her.

"Fuck y'all!" Rowdy said, still pouting but laughing.

*****

Kiara went to her job and started packing her things. She was so ready to put the life of a cop behind her. She went to talk to Detectives Moore and Carter, explaining to them that she was quitting. She told them that she was about to live her dream and sell real estate, and if they ever needed a house or property to contact her. The detectives wished her luck and didn't think much more of it.

She decided to take the box with her police things in it to her mother's house. She wanted to keep her past in the past. When she made it to her mother's house, she noticed that nobody was home. She grabbed her things and entered the house with her spare key and placed the box in her old room. Once the box was put away in the closet, she called Kaci to see if she wanted to meet for lunch.

"Hello," Kaci answered her phone.

"What's up, big head?!" Kiara shouted.

"Nothing, girl. What are you all excited about?" Kaci could tell that her friend was wired up, which was unusual.

"Nothing, I just wanted to see if you wanted to go eat."

Kaci said, "Not today, Kiara, I got a lot of work. But how about tomorrow?"

"Alright, but you bet not stand me up!"

"Bye, girl," Kaci said laughing, then hung up.

"Well, I guess I'll take my ass back home," Kiara told herself.

*****

"Ahh, shit!" Karbonado screamed. He had been going to therapy hours a day for two weeks, learning to walk again. He was making progress, but he was tired and felt like giving up. "Man, fuck this shit! Bring me that chair."

The physical therapist was used to difficult patients and wasn't offended by Karbonado's language. "Look, man, you can't give up. Come on." He was doing everything he could to encourage Karbonado.

"Look here, you pigskin smellin' motherfucka, bring me that fuckin' chair and roll me back to my room!" Karbonado yelled.

Figuring he had enough for one day, the therapist did as he was instructed without another word. He rolled Karbonado to his room and was walking out when Checkmate and Jania were coming in.

"How's he comin' along?" Checkmate asked.

121

"He's not trying to do anything. Every time he starts making progress, he gets mad and quits. He just yelled and cursed me out, telling me to bring him back to his room." Some of Karbonado's frustration was rubbing off on the therapist.

"Okay," Checkmate said, "I'll try to talk to him and see if I can help out."

"Thank you, ma'am."

Checkmate entered the room and found Karbonado sitting in a wheelchair sweating and drinking juice. He looked at Checkmate and felt embarrassed.

"Baby, why you not out doin' therapy?" she asked.

"Man, fuck that shit. Baby, go and buy me an electric wheelchair and take me home." He demanded it like a spoiled two year old.

"Boy, you have lost yo' fuckin' mind?" Checkmate echoed the same attitude he was dishing out. "Look, you need to quit actin' like a lil bitch and get your ass up and work out! It's been two weeks and you haven't gotten past the first stage of your recovery. Now you want me to help you stay cripple? Hell no, I'm not buyin' you no fuckin' electric chair, so get yo' lil bitch ass up and start walkin'!" He had picked the right one.

"Bitch, I'll swell yo' meat molestas up! What the fuck gave you the courage to say that? Bitch, you should be scared to talk to me like that!"

"Scared?" she asked as if it were a joke. "Nigga, you handicap. What the fuck can you do beside make threats?"

After she said that, Karbonado tried to jump out of his chair and grab her. But as soon as he jumped, she took a step back and he crashed to the floor. "Yeah, nigga, just like I thought! You can't even walk, but you wanna try to do something to somebody." Checkmate started walking toward the door. "Come on, Nia! " Unfortunately, Jania had seen the whole mess. She got up and made her way to the door.

"Do you think we should at least help him up?" she asked. Checkmate was tired of his mess and wasn't going to baby Karbonado anymore. "Hell no. When his stupid ass decide he's tired of bein' handicap, he will get up on his own. Let's go."

Jania felt sorry for him, but she knew Checkmate was serious.

They left the hospital and headed home. Both of them were quiet, lost in their own thoughts, until Jania started laughing.

"What the hell you laughin' about?" Checkmate asked.

"That nigga was gonna swell yo' meat molestas up!"

Checkmate giggled as well. "Girl, you know that nigga stupid. I just wish he would come on and get right. We been at war and I already gotta protect you. I can't afford to have to protect him as well."

Jania got serious. "Checkmate, I think you did go a lil hard on him."

"I know I did, but it's the truth. He just up. We have a baby on the way. I need him back up and runnin'."

Jania understood and made plans to help Checkmate in every way she could.

*****

Two days later, Karbonado finally convinced Checkmate to let him go home. He had even talked Rowdy into buying him an electric chair. All he wanted to do was lay down and watch television. Checkmate was mad and had been handling him rough, refusing to help him to the tub or do anything else he couldn't do for himself.

"Jania! Jania!" he called out.

She went to see what he wanted. "Why you yelling?" she asked Karbonado.

"Damn, why you actin' like you don't love me no more?" he asked in a sad tone.

Jania was standing in front of him with her hand covering her nose.

"I heard everything you used to say to me in that hospital, but now that I'm up, I don't feel none of the love you told me felt for me."

Jania removed her hand from her nose. "You wanna know the truth?" she asked.

"Yeah." he said, "Why wouldn't I want the truth? I'm a grown man."

"Look at you!" she said, frustrated. "You been here two days and haven't moved! You stink, you haven't bathed, you haven't brushed your teeth, you just fuckin' gave up! Don't nobody wanna sit with you and have to cover their nose the whole time! I do love you and Checkmate loves you! But no matter how much we love you, we will never love you more than you! Now when you ready to help yourself, I will help you, but I'm not about to keep babying you. You say you a man, then prove that to yourself 'cause I don't see the man I once knew!"

She stormed off. It hurt her to say these things to him, but they were the truth and he needed to hear them. She was mad because he gave up, not because he was still weak right now.

When she slammed the door to her bedroom, Karbonado felt the whole first floor shake. He knew she was pissed at him because she never cursed at him or raised her voice before. She had always done whatever she asked and now she was telling him no.

"Fuck!" he yelled, frustrated himself.

After sitting around feeling sorry for himself for an hour, he finally accepted the truth: He had given up and everything that Jania told him was real. He decided to start getting himself together.

"Jania! Janiaaa! Janiaaa!" he screamed.

She ran downstairs to see what he wanted. When she made it to the living room, she just looked at him and put her hand on her hip. "What do you want?" she asked with plenty of sarcasm.

"Can you get me some Gatorade out the refrigerator?"

She turned around, about to go back upstairs.

"I'm just playin'!" he yelled before she could leave. She stopped and turned around. "Look, you right, and I'm ready for you to help me."

She smiled and ran to hug him. "I hate seeing you like this!" she said and started crying.

Karbonado hugged her back and rubbed her shoulder. "I know, Nia. I was trippin'. Now go get the Gatorade so I can start trying to walk."

"No!" she said, once again covering her nose. "You need to bathe 'cause you gonna kill somebody with that smell if you add anymore sweat to your body."

"Fuck you, Nia!" he said and they both laughed. She helped him up and he rode to the bathroom himself. She ran his water and helped him take off his clothes.

"Look, I'm not bathing you," she said in all seriousness.

"I can bathe myself. I just need help getting in and out."

After he cleaned himself very well, Jania helped him get dressed. He was damn near looking like himself again once he shaved.

"Say," Jania said, "tomorrow, we will start walking. I don't want you to have to work out then have to take another bath."

" Okay, that do sound smart." He smiled at her. "Thank you, Nia. I love you. "

"I love you too. Now get your mind together because tomorrow we are going hard." She hoped he didn't take her warning lightly.

He laughed. "When is Checkmate comin' home?"

"She's not as long as you're not moving around. She hates seeing you like this. That's why she's been handlin' you the way she has. So we are not gonna tell her anything. Just get yourself together, and we'll surprise her."

Comfortable on the couch, Karbonado sat and talked to Jania like it was old times. She even rapped a few songs she wrote while he was gone.

"I'ma get you a studio built, and we startin a record label," Karbonado told Jania. She smiled, ready to go hard in the booth. She knew that she could be the queen of the south. And with Karbonado and his muscle and money, it wasn't a door she couldn't walk in.

*****

Karbonado and Jania had been working out for two hours a day for the past two weeks. He had finally gotten his legs back moving. They had started out taking baby steps and had progressed to running, jumping rope, squatting, and even doing pushups.

Checkmate had only been home twice, and she really believed that he wasn't moving from the couch. Jania and Karbonado had decided to trick her into coming home.

"Checkmate, this nigga threwed the remote and hit me in the face!" she yelled into the phone.

Checkmate told her she was on her way, and when she walked through the front door a few minutes later, she was out of breath from running from Rowdy's house. She walked up to Karbonado, who was sitting on the couch and slapped him.

"Nigga, have you lost yo' fuckin' mind throwin' shit at Nia? She been tryna help you and yo' ass actin' stupid!" She was screaming and pointing her finger in his face. She tried to slap him again when he just sat there looking stupid, but was shocked when he got up and pushed her down. Jania was standing on the side laughing 'cause Checkmate couldn't believe he was standing up. She now knew that they set her up.

"Get up, bad ass!" he yelled. "You was talkin' all that shit, a second ago!" He smiled at her. "Yeah, look at me now and come here and give me a hug 'cause I haven't seen you in weeks!"

Checkmate got up and just when he thought she was going to hug him, she slapped him again.

"Are you tryin' to kill our baby?" she yelled. "I told you about puttin' yo' hands on me!

"Bitch, you came in here hittin' me like this what you really want! I forgot about the baby." He lowered his head in guilt.

Jania was so happy to see them back fighting. She knew Karbonado was back and that Checkmate had been missing him as well. Everyone knew that they were one of those couples that were going to argue and fight damn near everyday, and they were all used to it.

"So how long you two been hidin' this shit from me?" Checkmate asked.

They explained how Jania handled him and how he was tired of being treated like a scrub and everyday they had started working out. Checkmate was so happy, she ran and called the twins and they both went to the house to see the brother who had finally returned to his old self.

CHAPTER 17

$$$

It took two months before everything was back to normal. Karbonado was back at the top of his game and was grinding nonstop. Checkmate was now five months pregnant and getting on his damn nerves.

"Damn, baby, when is you gonna spend time with me?" she complained. "All you been doin' is runnin' the streets!"

Karbonado sighed. "Baby, why you yellin'?" He was really trying to avoid a fight.

"'Cause I'm mad."

"Mad about what?"

She sat there for a minute to think about why she was mad and before she could answer, Karbonado said, "See, you don't even know why you mad!"

That's when she went crazy. "Nigga, I got these fuckin' babies in my stomach kickin' and rollin' around. You always gone and leavin' me by myself. I can't even spend time with Jania 'cause y'all always together.

Rowdy and Lil Moma been goin' out on dates with they new niggas so they ain't got time for me. I'm fat as hell and barely can breathe once I walk to the bathroom and back. And my feet are swole and you askin' why the fuck I'm mad?!" Of course, she screamed the whole two minutes she was talking, and Karbonado had put his hands over his ears because she was so loud.

"Baby," he said when she finally finished, "you trippin'. I just spent the whole day with you yesterday. And Jania been busy workin' on her mixtape. You know that damn girl love you."

"I can't tell she love me. She haven't stepped foot out that studio since you had it built for her." She pouted.

"Look, I'll tell you what. How 'bout you get dressed and I'll take you to the studio so y'all can spend some time together?"

"Okay, that sound cool, but at least call her and see if she want me to come hang out." She was definitely feeling like nobody wanted her around.

Karbonado shook his head at the silliness. "Just get dressed and I'll call her." He called and she answered on the second ring.

"Hey, daddy!"

"What's up? What are you doing?"

"I'm getting ready to spit some verses on that Mike Jones beat," she told him.

"Which one?"

"'Scandalous Hoes' and that 'Still Tippin' beat. I like those beats."

"Oh, okay. Well, look, yo' moma over here trippin'."

"What is she fussin' about? "Jania asked.

"She just tired of nobody wantin' to spend time with her, and she's talkin' about you don't love her and all this crazy shit."

"What? She knows I love her." Jania felt bad that Checkmate would even think something like that.

"Well, I asked if she wanted to spend time with you at the studio, and she said cool so I'm gonna bring her by."

"Okay, that's cool. What time are y'all coming?"

"We on our way as soon as yo' momma get dressed."

After they hung up, he waited on Checkmate to finish dressing so he could drop her off at the studio. While he was waiting, he thought about the day they decided to adopt Jania.

*****

Two months earlier, Karbonado and Checkmate had been in the bed talking when he decided it was time to address their long-term plans for Jania. He was back up and running, but what had happened reminded him that life was short.

"Baby, I know when you first brought Jania over I was a asshole. but after all these months, I have grown to love her and I want to ask you how do you feel about adoptin' her."

Checkmate looked at him and smiled. "I'm okay with that, but it's not just about what we want. We have to sit and talk to her and see how she feel about all this."

"Janiaaa, Janiaaa!" he yelled.

She walked into the room and held her hands over her ears.

"Why are you yelling?" she asked. Checkmate started laughing.

"Jania, we wanted to ask you how you felt about us adoptin' you?" Karbonado asked.

Jania's face lit up, and she ran and took a dive in the bed, hugging both of them tightly. "I'll love that. When can we do it?"

"Well, we have to get yo' momma to sign some papers sayin' she's okay with givin' you up for adoption," Checkmate explained.

Jania put her head down. "I guess we can forget about that then. "

130

"No, we will not forget about nothin'. We gonna go by her spot and I'll give her money to sign you over to me. She's a drug addict, trust me, she not gonna turn down free money." It was a shame that it was true, but Karbonado knew he was right, as was proven a few days later when she sold Jania for $1,200.

*****

"Boy, you ready?" Checkmate asked, bringing him back to reality.

"Damn, girl, you wearin' that pink sundress! Keep it up and I'ma have to hit that before we go." He slapped her on the ass.

"Nigga, please! I ain't lettin' you put nothin' else of yours in me. I call myself bein' nice by givin' you a lil pussy and now I'm stuck carryin' twins!" She laughed as she pushed him towards the door.

They left the house and got in the car, driving to the new studio that Karbonado had built for Jania. When they got there, Jania was hanging outside, hugged up with Trigga. Karbonado hadn't met Trigga so he was pissed. He got out of the car and walked straight to Jania.

"Daddy, this is Trigga," she introduced with a smile.

Karbonado wasn't trying to hear it. "Why the hell you got yo' hands on my daughter's ass? Nigga, have you lost yo' fuckin' mind?" he yelled, snatching Trigga's hand off Jania.

Jania just backed up and let Trigga explain. "Look, Mr. Karbonado, no disrespect. I got respect for yo' daughter and I apologize if you felt disrespected."

Karbonado pulled his gun out and placed it to the top of his head. "Nigga, if you don't get yo' lil punk ass out my face and out this parkin' lot, I'm gonna pop yo' fuckin' top!"

Trigga turned around, and he and his homeboy got in the car and left.

131

"Daddy, why did you do that?" Jania asked, mad and embarrassed .

"If you gonna bring a nigga around me, bring somebody that can protect you. Lil bitch ass nigga wouldn't stand up for his self, fuck make you think he gonna stand up for you? We don't need no weak links in our family, Jania!" He fussed some more and then walked inside the studio.

Jania was still mad though, because she really liked Trigga. "Mama, Daddy trippin'!" she screamed.

"Nia, as much as I hate to agree with him, he's right. You know the type of lifestyle we live. He need to be able to know that if y'all are out, Trigga will be able to protect you. What if someone disrespected you? He wouldn't even stand up for his self. You know how yo' daddy is. So find you a standup nigga." Checkmate walked off, too.

Jania felt bad, but she had to admit her parents were right. And she could only ride with what they said. She walked back into the studio and started listening to her latest verse.

"You still mad at me?" Karbonado asked when she was in the studio.

She looked at him and rolled her eyes. "You know I can't stay mad at you," she said and smiled.

"Good, now keep yo' momma company while I hit these streets," he said, running out of the studio.

She just laughed and started playin' her latest songs for Checkmate.

CHAPTER 18

$$$

Kiara was having the best time of her life. She and Damn Fool were now living together and expecting a baby. She had been doing good with flipping properties through High Rise Real Estate, a company that Damn Fool started but incorporated in Lil D's name. As the CEO of Dawg House Records, Lil D had legitimate cash and everything would look above board. The truth, however, was that despite the fact that the incorporation papers said that Lil D owned 60% and Kiara 40% of the company, Lil D's 60% belonged to Damn Fool and Karbonado.

The plan was for Karbonado to build his music label, then, after two years, he would buy the real estate company from Lil D. All of this under the table stuff was to stop anybody from believing that anything illegal was going on, while Karbonado laundered drug money through the real estate company and washed it clean.

"Baby, guess what?" Kiara asked Damn Fool.

"What's up?"

"You're not gonna believe this, but Kaci is pregnant." She laughed.

"Why is it funny, though?" he asked.

She looked at him for a second. "'Cause she's pregnant by Karbonado!" she told him and started laughing again.

"What?! Hell nah, you lyin'. Why he ain't told me about this?"

"He don't know she's pregnant. She's too embarrassed to tell him. "

"Well, she better hope Checkmate don't kill her." And he wasn't doing no laughing when he said it.

"Baby, those three had a threesome, and she ended up pregnant," she told him.

"Damn! Yo' girl a freak like that?!" he asked, shocked.

"No. I don't know how he talked her into it. But that's what happened and now she's pregnant and ashamed to tell him. And what's so funny is she hadn't had none in almost two years and when she finally got some dick she got pregnant." Kiara shook her head in amazement.

"So when she plan on tellin' him 'cause you know he about to ask Checkmate to marry him on Mother's Day, right?"

"Damn! I didn't know that, but I'ma suggest she tell him asap." Kiara picked up the phone to call Kaci. While the phone was ringing, she noticed the smile on Damn Fool's face. "By the way," she said, waiting until he looked at her to continue, "I know what you are thinking, and you might as well forget it. I don't do threesomes."

Damn Fool chuckled, and said, "It don't hurt a brotha to dream a little."

＊＊＊＊＊

Kaci had just got off the phone with Kiara, and she was now encouraged to tell Karbonado. She picked up the phone and dialed his number.

134

"What's up, sexy?" he answered.

"Nothing, are you busy?"

"I'm never too busy to talk to you," Karbonado responded.

"I want to meet up with you. Is that cool?"

"Yeah, what you got in mind, the Moezy Rozy?" he asked playfully.

She laughed. The Moezy Rozy was a reference to a hotel in the movie *The Player's Club*. "Boy, you nasty! No, I need to holla at you about something important, so let's meet real quick."

After talking for another ten minutes, they agreed to get together at The Cheesecake Factory. Upon arriving, they went inside and got a table. Kaci decided to just jump in and get in over with.

"Karbonado, you got me pregnant."

He looked at her closely before responding. He had women try to pull same bullshit on him before, but he could see fear in her eyes and knew she was serious. "So what you lookin' so worried about? If it's mine, then I'ma take care of y'all. It ain't no point in cryin' about spilled milk, literally."

"Boy, why you always playin'? Here I am trying to be serious and you being nasty again." She did smile and let out a sigh, relieved that he didn't trip about it. But there was still another issue. "You're cool with this, but what about your girl? I mean, how do you think she's going to react?"

"Well, she been bitchin' about everything since she been pregnant. But what can we do? What's done is done. I hate to tell her this, but somebody gotta tell her."

"Well let me know how it turns out, 'cause I got room on my couch if you need a place to sleep," she joked.

"Ha, ha. You the one should find the place you want to rest in peace. And besides that, you know damn well if I stay with you won't be no sleepin' on no couch." He winked at her.

135

"Whatever," Kaci said, getting up to leave. "Call me later when she put you out."

* * * * *

"This boy will not stop calling!" Jania complained. "Momma, what do you think about the song I just played?"

Checkmate rubbed her belly, and said, "I like it. I think that's gonna have the radio jumpin'.

While they were listening to some music, someone kicked the door open.

Checkmate and Jania jumped. "Trigga, what are you doing?" Jania asked when he walked into the room. She was scared as hell, watching Trigga point a 45 Desert Eagle at the head of one of the bodyguards.

"The only reason I let that shit ride earlier was out of respect for you and yo' mama. Yo' daddy think I'm soft, but here's a wake-up call!"

He shot the body guard twice in the head.

"Nigga, you got to be one stupid, crazy, gangsta, son of a bitch!" Checkmate yelled.

"Tell yo' daddy I already took care of the other two body guards. So he ain't gotta get his hands dirty. I was taught to never pull yo' strap out and not use it." He looked at both of the women and walked out. In the other room, he walked up to the other two bodyguards who were still knocked out, finished his work, and left.

Checkmate called Karbonado to let him know what had just happened. "What's up, baby?"

"You need to come to the studio, asap!" she shouted.

"Damn, baby," he said concerned, "What you trippin' 'bout now?"

"That nigga you pulled yo' gun on came back up here and killed all three bodyguards! You need to get here now!" She hung up the phone.

"Momma, I'm sorry. I didn't know he would do something so stupid."

"Jania, it's too late to be sorry. You brought that nigga over here and he violated. Look!" she said, pointing at the dead body. "That nigga killed three matherfuckas! It could have been me, the babies, and yo' dumb ass!" Checkmate was so angry all she could do was walk off to keep from slapping Jania.

Jania was devastated and began crying because she never had any idea things could get so messed up, which was what kids didn't understand about relationships.

Twenty minutes later, Karbonado showed up with six of his goons. He couldn't believe he had underestimated Trigga. He and Jania both had made a mistake. "Y'all clean this shit up," he ordered his crew. He walked back to talk to Checkmate, who was yelling orders over the phone.

"I need to see you right now, and bring T-Rich with you and Chico!" she told her right hand man J.C. Through giving orders, she turned and saw Karbonado standing there.

"Fuck you lookin' at me like this shit my fault?" she yelled.

"I ain't say shit. All I did was look at you, but if we talkin' about who's at fault, it is yo' fault! You got these weak ass bodyguards that could have cost you and our kids their life!" He was speaking the truth quite loudly, and Checkmate couldn't deny what he was saying.

"You right, I fucked up and I'm goin' to fix this shit. I had a lot on my plate when you was gone. That's why I had Chico put together some shooters. But I'm gonna make it right!" she said walking off. Jania heard the whole argument and felt bad that she was the reason. "Let's go, Jania!" They walked to Karbonado's Range Rover and Jania juststood there.

"Is Daddy coming?" Jania asked, wanting to know if she was riding shotgun or not.

"No, he's catchin' a ride with one of his boys," she answered, rubbing her belly again.

"You alright?" Jania asked with concern after she saw her momma make a funny face.

"Yeah," Checkmate said, "these girls act like they fightin' over me." She laughed.

During the ride back home, Checkmate got a call from J.C. letting her know that he had T-Rich and Chico with him. She ordered him to meet her at the warehouse they usually held meetings at. He was to show up at 6PM with the rest of the crew.

CHAPTER 19

$$$

It was 6:00 and the Black Diamond Cartel members were all at the warehouse, waiting on Checkmate and Karbonado. Rowdy and Lil Moma were already there. At 6:05 they finally showed up. He and Checkmate surprised everyone because they never brought Jania around when they needed to discuss problems.

Jania was shocked to see so many people, realizing she had never seen most of them before. She stood stuck in place as her mom and dad greeted everyone.

After they all spoke to one another, the meeting began. The group was updated on the events of the day, and Checkmate then asked D.C. to bring out Chico and T-Rich. Everyone was shocked to see Chico beat the hell up. T-Rich didn't understand what he had done, but he soon found out when D.C. brought his baby brother, Trigga out.

Checkmate yelled at Chico, "You see this one, motherfucka?" She pointed at Trigga. "He managed to get past three bodyguards that you brought in this family! And not only did he get past them, he killed them and could have killed me, my twins, and Jania!

"Lucky for us, he just wanted to prove a point, and in a way, I'm glad he did. 'Cause now I know that I'm not safe with the guys you assigned to protect us." Not many of them had ever seen Checkmate this angry before. "Jania, come here," she demanded of her daughter. Jania slowly shuffled over to Checkmate, tears rolling down her cheeks.

"In this family," Checkmate said, lifting her chin up so she could look her in the eye, "we have rules, and one of the rules is that you are responsible far who you bring into this family. You are responsible for who you bring around this family.

"I brought in Chico and he brought in those three that's dead. And I brought you in! I'm responsible for you two. And because of you, I have three dead guards. You brought this nigga around us, so you're responsible for his actions."

She handed Jania her 9mm. Jania wouldn't take the gun, simply staring at it. Checkmate grabbed her hand and stuck the pistol in it. "You about to turn 17, and you are not about to place my life or your sisters' life in danger again." She pointed at Chico. "Kill him and you better empty the clip," she demanded.

Jania looked at her mother, the tears on her face heavy, and shook her head no.

Checkmate smirked and pulled out her .357, placing it to her daughter's head. Jania's eyes got as big as golf balls. "You either take responsibility for yo' fuck up, or you can die right here with Chico. I don't give a fuck about you bein' my daughter 'cause yo' daddy don't give a fuck about me bein' his kids' mother. He will kill me if I don't take responsibility for the people I brought in, pregnant or not."

Jania understood for the first time how real this shit was. She lifted the gun up to Chico's head and after a quick thought she knew her momma was dead serious. It was either kill or be killed because Checkmate wasn't about to give someone the opportunity to kill her or the twins.

And Karbonado didn't bend the rules when it came to the Black Diamond Cartel.

Jania closed her eyes and put sixteen shots in Chico's body, most of them after he was already dead. Checkmate took the gun from her trembling hand and told her to get in the car. In the car, she cried and cried. She couldn't believe that her mother was so mad at her that she had made her kill Chico.

"Now, T-Rich, you didn't bring yo' brother around us and that's why you're alive, but I'm not gonna just let him make it. You still gotta pay for his actions," Checkmate told him. She looked at J.C. and he began beating him so bad his brother begged Checkmate to call him off. She told J.C. to stop. "We family and this is what I call tough love. Next time, think before you react 'cause it's real over here."

J.C. began to beat the shit out of Trigga, but after about two minutes, Karbonado ordered him to stop. He walked up to Trigga, and even though Trigga's eyes were swollen, he still looked Karbonado in the eyes. "I got a lot of respect for you. I know you knew about me and what I would do to you. But you still showed up and showed me you would rather die for respect. As you can see, in this family we take responsibility for our actions. My daughter ain't never killed nobody, but once she brought you around, you became her responsibility. The only reason she killed Chico instead of you is because I decided to offer you a spot in my family. What do you say?"

"What happen if I decline yo' offer, I'll die right here?" Trigga asked.

"No," Karbonado told him. "If you decline my offer, you walk out alive and nobody from my family will touch you. But if you ever violate my family again, then I will kill you and everyone you love. I promise you that."

Trigga had to admit that he was standing in a room full of killas, and everyone seemed loyal to each other. He also liked how they were organized. "Yeah, I'll accept a spot at your family table," he said, shaking Karbonado's hand.

Jania watched the whole thing from the car, confused because she couldn't understand why her parents didn't kill him after he put down some members of the Black Diamond Cartel.

*****

It had been a few days since Jania caught her first body. She was so mad at her parents that she refused to talk to them. Everyday, she got up and got ready for school and waited outside for Checkmate to drop her off.

On the third day, Checkmated decided to let her have it. "So, you gonna wake up everyday and not speak to me?" Jania ignored her and that caused Checkmate to blank out. She walked to the passenger side of the car and snatched Jania by her hair, pulling her out of the car.

"Bitch, you got a problem, then get it off yo' chest. I kissed yo' ass and accepted yo' attitude for two days. I'm not goin' for a third day!" she yelled, out of breath, but still holding on to Jania by her hair.

Jania was crying hard when she answered. "I didn't want to become a killer, and you forced me to be that! Why, Momma, why?" Checkmate was hurting for her daughter, but she refused to allow Jania to get her caught up in stupid situations. "Jania, you almost 17. The lifestyle me and yo' daddy live is nothin' to play about. I needed you to understand that you have to think before you do certain things. What if Trigga would've shot me and killed these twins?"

"I understand, Momma, but y'all let him live and killed Chico," she said, slamming her hand on the hood of the car, breaking a nail in the process.

"We killed Chico because he put our life in danger. He assigned those bodyguards. If they were on point, then Trigga would of never made it past them. Trigga killed those other two because he already knew that your daddy was gonna kill them. And that's what yo' daddy and I respected.

"He's not soft. He's a killer and we decided he needed to be on our team. His brother didn't get killed 'cause he's not the one who brought him around. You did. So now you understand that you need to know who you dealin' with. And if you do bring someone around, then it's yo' responsibility to keep them in line."

Jania said she understood, and they hugged. "I love you, Momma!"

"I love you, too, Nia. Now let's get you to school before you be late." Checkmate tried to walk fast but had to stop to catch her breath.

"Fat self. How were you gonna fight me and you get tired just taking two steps?"

They both started laughing.

Chapter 20

$$$

A week later, Karbonado and Checkmate were at the house spending time together when he decided to break the news. "Baby, I got something to tell you."

"What's up?" she asked, looking at him crazy.

"Kaci called me and said that she's pregnant by me."

Checkmate sat up in bed and looked at him, wanting to make sure she heard him correctly. "What you say?" she asked.

Karbonado prepared himself for the storm then repeated what he had said, after which she flipped out. "Nigga, what the fuck you mean she pregnant by you?! I can't believe this shit. I already gotta deal with these two motherfuckas in my stomach. Now you talkin' about another bitch and a baby. I can't believe you!" She stood up and threw the magazine she had been reading, then she started to walk out of the room.

"Baby, you act like it's all my fault! It was yo' idea from the jump. You told me I could pick any bitch and we would have a threesome!" He was yelling too, mad because he should have known this shit was going to come back on him somehow.

"But I ain't say nut in the bitch!" She started crying. "You know what? Fuck it. I can't even be mad. It's my fault. You right about that." She left the room.

Karbonado was about to follow her but decided it was probably best to give her time alone.

*****

"Niaa!" Checkmate yelled from the bottom of the stairs.

Jania came out of her room to the staircase. "What's up, Momma? " she asked.

"You wanna ride with me?"

"Yeah, let me put my shoes on." Jania started to walk off, then stopped and asked, "Wait, where we going?"

"To find you another daddy!" she screamed.

"And when you do, you better find another continent to live on," Karbonado responded.

Jania shook her head and started laughing because she knew they were at it again. Whenever they fought, Checkmate always asked her to ride with her, and they would end up getting some ice cream. She ran to grab her phone and put her shoes on.

When she was in the car and they were leaving the estate, Jania decided to be nosy. "Momma, what y'all fighting about now?" she asked, laughing.

"This nigga got another bitch pregnant. Now he puttin' the blame all on me. Stupid ass nigga should've put some protection on!"

"So what's gonna happen now?" This was more serious than Jania realized.

"I don't know," Checkmate admitted.

"Well you know Daddy loves you, so don't let that destroy what y'all built," she told her mother.

"We good. I can't even be mad."

Jania didn't understand what she meant by that. She would definitely be mad if her man got another woman pregnant. But she left it alone, not wanting to upset her mother more than she already was.

While they were driving, Checkmate sent a text to Kaci asking if they could meet up. She was surprised when Kaci texted her back with an invitation to come by her house, which Checkmate wasted no time doing.

When they got there, Jania was curious. "Who lives here?"

"Kaci," Checkmate said. "Come on."

As they got out of the car, Jania dropped her head and shook it. She just knew her mother was about to kill Kaci, but was shocked when Kaci opened the door and Checkmate hugged her as if nothing had happened.

Kaci had Kiara and Damn Fool over and they both greeted Checkmate and Jania. Kaci had asked them to come because she didn't know what would happen between her and Checkmate.

"Can we go somewhere private and talk?" Checkmate asked.

"Yeah, let's go in my room," Kaci responded.

They both walked into the room, and Damn Fool, Kiara, and Jania were waiting to hear them tearing the room up.

"Look, Kaci, we grown. I can't be mad about you gettin' pregnant 'cause shit happen. But this is what I do know: Karbonado is both our baby daddy. I know he gonna be comin' over here sneakin' and fuckin' you every chance he get. And you will get to the point where you try to make him choose between me and you. But I'm not goin' nowhere, and I'm damn sure not lettin ' him go anywhere. So to keep me from killin' y'all, I suggest we become one big happy family."

Kaci wasn't sure she was comprehending Checkmate right. Not only had she made the suggestion, but she did it with a smile on her face. "What do you mean become a big happy family?" she asked, obviously shocked.

"Look, let's keep it 100. Karbonado is attracted to you. We both know that and vice versa. That's why he picked you out of all people to have a threesome with. Now I'm all about makin' my nigga happy, 'cause I don't believe in givin' the next bitch that chance. And honestly, I enjoyed our night together. I could tell it was your first time cummin the way you did when I ate that pussy." Checkmate was looking her in the eyes, with a smirk on her face as she said it.

"Look, Checkmate, I am attracted to Karbonado, and that's why I did what I did. I had never done anything like that and I enjoyed it. I'm not gonna lie." She rubbed her head.

"Understand this," Checkmate said, "if me and him together, then he's gonna cheat on me with you and vice versa. I don't want to wake up mad 'cause I feel he's out with you. And I don't want you to go through that either. Because that's goin' to bring tension between us, and you know how I am," she said with very clear meaning.

"You right, and I feel the same." Kaci took a deep breath, not even knowing how she got herself in this mess. "I don't want to raise my child without a father in the house. Asia already doesn't have a father figure."

"So let's make this work because we are two queens fit for one king," Checkmate said with a smile.

"So not only will I be Karbonado's bitch, but I'm your bitch too?" she asked, laughing.

"And vice versa," Checkmate told her then kissed her on the lips. "Now go pack a few clothes and meet me at the house at seven tonight. I would love to surprise our baby daddy." They both laughed at this.

Thirty minutes after they had gotten there, Checkmate and Jania left to go get ice cream before going back home.

What none of them could believe was that Kaci was still alive and breathing when Checkmate walked out of the door.

CHAPTER 21

$$$

Karbonado, Checkmate, and Kaci were in the bed asleep when Jania came and woke them up with the twins crying.

"Damn, Nia, you couldn't put their ass back to sleep?" Checkmate said getting up.

"Momma, you act like I got some titties full of milk!"

"You better watch yo' smart lil mouth, girl." Checkmate was laughing when she said it.

It had been a month since she gave birth to the twins, Diamond and Princess. Karbonado was more than happy because he knew that he could finally have a lil peace. And a lot of fun.

Ever since Kaci had moved in five months earlier, the two women had been tag-teaming him, and he couldn't decide what was the problem—until Rowdy explained that it was the babies.

Kaci, who could barely move she was so big, said, "Let me see Princess." She was due the next month and Karbonado couldn't wait to have a son. Kaci seemed to adapt to being in a relationship with another

149

woman, and she was surprised that she was actually stress-free. She and Checkmate shared a strong bond and would sometimes stay up late, cuddling and talking. Karbonado didn't understand how Checkmate, out of the blue, became so into another woman.

He was at the mall with Rowdy when he expressed himself.

"I think the pregnancy made my girl a straight freak!"

"Why you say that?" Rowdy asked, looking at him crazy.

"'Cause that night at my party, we were chillin' in VIP and she just out of the blue told me to pick any bitch in the club, so we could go home and toss her up. So I picked Kaci, and when we got her to come back to the house, she just went pussy crazy! I mean she had her ass in a lock and damn near sucked Kaci dry, and—"

"—Hey, hey, hey. I don't need to hear all y'all details!" She plugged up her ears with her fingers, and Karbonado laughed. "Look, bro, Checkmate been into girls. Ever since we were in the twelfth grade. Before you, she hadn't been with a nigga in two years. And for some reason, she just went left and fell in love with you." Rowdy shrugged her shoulders. "So you better enjoy the best of both worlds 'cause it's a lot of niggas wish they could be yo' shoes!"

Karbonado agreed. Here he was watching both of his baby mamas care for his twins. Kaci and Princess seemed to get along well. There were times when Checkmate couldn't get her to stop crying, but when Kaci came around she was all happy. Most of the time, Checkmate had Diamond with her.

Jania was really enjoying playing with her sisters. She would take them into her room and allow them to sleep with her at night.

"Can y'all hoes shut up!" Karbonado complained. "It's two in the morning!"

"Hoes!" all three of them shouted.

150

That's when he knew he had fucked up. "Y'all know what I mea—"
He was cut short.

Whop!

Kaci slapped him. "Nigga, you got me fucked up." Hanging around
Checkmate had definitely made Miss Prim and Proper a lot more
gangsta. "Matter fact…" She pushed him out of the bed and he hit the
floor. "…Take yo' ass and go sleep on the couch!" Kaci yelled.

Jania tried to hold in her laughter, but her attempt failed. Karbonado
got up pissed and went straight to his closet and got a belt. "I told you
about that bullshit," he said, about to hit Kaci with the belt.

"Nigga, if you hit my girl with that belt, I swear on my kids I'm
gonna shoot yo' ass!" Checkmate warned him, and he knew she was
serious.

"Fuck all y'all!" he shouted, then left the room mad as hell.

"Stupid motherfucka lost his mind," Checkmate said. "Here, hold
Diamond," she told Jania.

Checkmate passed Diamond to Jania and put her titty back in her
bra, then went to the living room. Karbonado had just laid on the couch
and was about to smoke a blunt. When he saw Checkmate, he let out
a long sigh, not really interested in round two, but knowing she was
going to speak her mind anyway.

"Nigga, I thought you was better than that!" she yelled at him.

"You already said what you had to say, now go feed the twins
because they are hungry," he told her, trying to end a losing battle.

"Yeah, whatever," Checkmate snarled, "you just tryna get out of
what yo' silly ass just did." When he didn't respond, she walked out of
the living room to feed the kids.

CHAPTER 22

$$$

It was another exciting day for Karbonado. A month after he had nearly spanked Kaci, she gave birth to his son. He sat down beside her hospital bed, holding his son in his arms. He had decided to name the baby Jaylen Lewis, proud to be the one who determined what the boy would be called for the rest of his life.

While he was holding his son, Checkmate and his sisters rumbled through the door with a boatload of gifts. "Damn, why y'all bring all that shit up here?!" he asked, knowing they were going to overdo it, and also knowing there was nothing he could do to stop them.

Rowdy said, "I got some fly shit for my nephew." She began pulling out outfits as if he was going to wear one right then.

Karbonado just shook his head, pissed because when it was time to leave, he would be the one carrying all of that shit out of the hospital and back into the house.

Kaci was really enjoying the love that the twins and Checkmate showered her with. Baby J.C. assigned two bodyguards to go with Jania to buy her outfit for her birthday party.

Checkmate told him, "That ain't til next month, but I don't think we should let her have that party. I want to take her and her friends to Miami. We got too much goin' on down here to let our guard down. I mean think about it, Young Hogg been too quiet." Checkmate thought about what he said and had to admit he was right. Young Hogg hadn't been making a sound, which only meant that he was plotting. They both knew it wasn't because he was afraid of them.

"So who's goin' to break the news to Nia?" Checkmate asked. "Me or you?"

"Kaci," Karbonado responded innocently.

"You a lie," Kaci said laughing.

They both knew how he hated to disappoint her, but they knew the party wouldn't be a good idea. It would give Hogg too much of an opportunity.

*****

Jania, Cornbread, Cupcake, and Darkskin were all at the Galleria Mall, shopping for Jania's seventeenth birthday party. They decided to go inside the Louis Vuitton store and that's when she met P. Diamonds, a 17-year-old Haitian from Miami who transported drugs for some dread heads in Lil Haiti. P. Diamonds noticed Jania and was making his way over to her when he was stopped by the two big bodyguards.

"Woah! Slow ya roll, lil daddy," one of the bodyguards told him.

"Damn Debo, calm down. I'm just tryin' to holla at the beautiful lady in the white," he said, pointing at Jania.

Torch looked at Jania, and she gave him some advice. "You know the rule, Torch. Pat him down." She had learned a valuable lesson from dealing with Trigga, and now she had a number one rule. If you want to go near those four ladies, then you have to be pat searched." Torch told P. Diamonds the rule, and he could only stare at the girls, who continued to pick through the different clothes and shoes. At that moment, he knew that the girl in the white wasn't the average damsel.

He held his arms out and allowed Torch to pat him down, after which he was allowed to speak with the girls. "Damn, I feel like I just entered the airport!" P. Diamonds said with a smile. The girls looked at him and laughed.

"Well then you should always feel safe when you are in the presence of us." Jania said, pointing to her three friends. "Now where are you from, what's your name, and what do you do for a living?" she asked.

"Damn, who you work for HPD or the feds?" he asked, laughing again showing off his pretty white teeth.

"Neither. I just need to know who I'm dealin' with. So either you answer me, or you can move around 'cause you interruptin' my shoppin' spree," she told him with more than a little ghettotude.

"Damn, you feisty!" he said before answering the questions. "First, I'm from Miami. Second, my name is P. Diamonds. And third, I spend a lot of my time traveling back and forth between Miami and Houston." He had raised up one finger to begin with, then another as he ticked off each answer. "Now, did I answer all of your inquiries, madam?" he asked in a butchered English accent.

He hadn't, and she figured he was a drug dealer, but for now she wouldn't reveal her knowledge of the game. She would play lame for now.

"I hear you got an accent," she said, not answering the question. "Are you a Jamaican?" Despite the sorry accent he had tried to speak with, she could hear the soft island tone.

154

P. Diamonds looked at her with great offense. "I'm Haitian, not Maician. That's an insult to call a Haitian Jamaican and vice versa."

"Well, as you see, I didn't mean any disrespect. So what's up? Why are you in my space? You gonna get my number or continue to interrupt my shoppin'?"

He laughed and asked for her number.

"How old are you?" she asked.

"I'm 17. What about you?"

Jania said, "I'm about to turn 17 next month. Is that a problem?"

He smiled that big, pretty smile. "Damn, you a baby. I guess we could be friends until you turn 18!"

Jania just shook her head at his silliness. She gave him the number, and said, "Don't tell me you goin' to call and don't. Now let me get back to spending my time with my girls." She waved bye and walked off to shop with her friends, who had moved over a few aisles to give them some privacy once they started talking.

P. Diamonds was really feeling her style. He liked how she handled herself like a boss and he planned on calling her real soon.

When he walked off, Cornbread said, "Damn, that nigga fine as hell!" She didn't even give Jania time to say a word before she started going off about how good P. Diamonds looked.

"You are right about that," Jania admitted, "but we may never talk like that once I check his background."

"Why you say that?" Darkskin asked.

"Because I know he's a drug dealer," Jania responded.

Cupcake crinkled her eyes. "And what's wrong with that? Yo' parents are the biggest dope dealers in the city," she said, laughing.

"And that's the problem," Jania said, shaking her head as if dealing with uninformed children. "He's from Miami and he said he travels back and forth from there and here. Plus, he's only 17 and got on more ice than Lil Boosie, which means he's running drugs down for somebody.

"And that's a violation to my family, 'cause nobody down here sells anything unless they buy from my fam."

"Jania, just 'cause he's icy don't mean he's a drug dealer," Cornbread said. "He could be a jack boy or the son of a celebrity. Don't just judge the nigga. Look at us, we ain't hoes, boosters, or drug dealers, but we stay drippin' in the best shit money can buy."

Jania said, "You right, so instead of me assuming, I'm gonna holla at him and get to know him." She stopped talking about it after that, and her friends knew the conversation was finished concerning P. Diamonds. "Y'all ready?" Jania asked.

"Yeah, I can't wait to jump in this shit," Cornbread said.

They all had some fly shit and were now ready to hit the house.

*****

It had been a few months since Young Hogg had been in Houston. He had taken his kids, wife, and niece to Louisiana because he wanted them to be safe. Now he had a plan, and he was getting ready to cause the Black Diamond Cartel a whole lot of hell.

Checkmate had showed him that she was a certified killer to the max. He knew that he had to touch her where it would hurt her the most. He was trying to find out her family background, but so far he had come up empty.

Young Hogg had been in the game for a while and he had a bunch of connects. He called in a few boyz from New Orleans to help him wipe out Karbonado and his family. He promised them half of their turf once they were all dead, and that's all it took. The Body Snatchers accepted the contract.

156

The Body Snatchers were a group of ten contract killers. Young Hogg gave them the name and plugged them in with a lot of big money people who were always looking to pay to have someone they had beef with killed. He knew without a doubt they could handle Checkmate and he planned on making her pay for killing his family.

Hogg was getting ready to go back to Houston and show the Black Diamond Cartel he was the man everyone should fear. The Body Snatchers were already on their way and they couldn't wait to spill blood.

CHAPTER 23

$$$

Two weeks later, Jania had been at the studio working on her mixtape when she invited P. Diamonds over and found out that he knew how to produce. He put together a track for her and she came up with a song called "Too Bossy." While finishing her adlibs, her parents walked in.

"Hey, Momma, what's up?"

"Nothing, yo' daddy wanted to stop over here and see how yo' mixtape comin' out," Checkmate answered and sat on the couch.

Her father also walked up, and she introduced P. Diamonds.

"Daddy, this P. Diamonds, the one I told you about."

"What's up wit' it?" Karbonado asked, sticking out his hand.

Jania was surprised at the way her father greeted P. Diamonds. She had never seen him so relaxed around new people and that told Jania that her father had taken a liking to P. Diamonds off the top.

"Where you from, P. Diamonds?" Karbonado asked.

"I'm from Miami, Carol City," he answered with pride.

Karbonado said, "I got some people out there, too. You know Diamond Dawg?"

"I don't know him personally, but I heard of him. He's a legend and run Miami."

"Let me ask you something, P. Diamonds." Karbonado said, looking the kid straight in the eye. "Could I come to Miami and post up and sell work on Diamond Dawg turf?"

P. Diamonds wasn't sure where he was going, but he answered anyway. "No, not unless you a part of his team."

Karbonado, never taking his eyes of P. Diamonds, asked, "Are you a part of my team?"

P. Diamonds frowned. "No, I don't even know you. I never even heard of you until now."

Karbonado got that tense smile on his face. "Have you heard of the Black Diamond Cartel?"

"Hell, yeah!" P. Diamonds said. "They ruthless and ran by some bitch name Checkmate."

The moment he said the words, Jania knew it was over. Checkmate walked over to him and pulled her gun out and placed it to his head. "Nigga, who you callin' a bitch?"

By this time, everything began to make sense. He had been bringing drugs to Houston for six months for some Haitians out of Miami. He didn't know that he was in the wrong because he got paid to drive, and the niggas he was bringing drugs to were from Houston.

"I'm gonna ask you one time, who are you bringin' dope to out here?" Checkmate asked.

"Look, I respect you and yo' family," P. Diamonds said, not showing any fear, "but I rather die than snitch. That's not in my blood. I'm Diamonds. How about I take you to the man I'm driving for and let him tell you?"

"Oh, we already know who you work for." Checkmate had not moved the gun away from his head yet. "Just do me a favor?" she asked.

"What's that? "

"I respect how you handled yo' self and because of that, I'ma let you live and pretend this never happened. But don't ever bring no drugs to my city unless it's for us.

"And, by the way, Day Money got killed for disrespecting us." She let her gun hand fall and walked away, Karbonado with her.

Day Money was, or had been, the man P. Diamonds was moving drugs for. P. couldn't believe that the girl he met in the mall was tied in with someone so ruthless.

"You set me up!" he said.

"Boy, didn't nobody set you up, 'cause if I did you would be dead," she informed him.

"Then why did they show up? How they know I was over here?"

Jania sighed. "First off, calm your ass down. Those are my parents, and I told them about you 'cause I need to know who I'm dealing with, and my parents are well-connected. If you was considered the enemy, then you would be dead. And to let you in on a secret, you the first boy I ever brought around that my dad shook hands with. So if you wanna move around, then leave. Or we can continue to build a friendship."

P. Diamonds really did like Jania, despite what had happened. She was smart and sexy and he loved her boss attitude. "I see where you get yo' bossy attitude from," he said then gave her a hug.

After an hour of working on her mixtape, Jania called Torch to tell him she would be ready to leave soon. She found out that her parents were still at the studio in her father's office.

P. was getting ready to leave, but Karbonado pulled him into his office to talk to him. "P. Diamonds, I hope you didn't take it personal earlier. But just like Diamond Dawg, I have rules down here too. I

160

understand you haven't heard of me, but that's only because I laid up in the ICU for a while." He paused and lifted his shirt to show P. his bulletwound. "Now, I can tell you really like my daughter. But I know you can't provide for her, and I understand why. So I'm gonna open the door for you to get major money with my team. I already checked yo' background, and I know everything about you. And you can thank Diamond Dawg, because he's the reason Checkmate didn't put yo' lights out."

"Mr. Karbonado, I'm proud and honored for the opportunity to be a part of yo' team. But what is it that I'm gonna do?"

Karbonado smiled at him. "I need some shooters, and I'm talkin' ruthless killers. Some hungry motherfuckas that want to eat and feed their family. Some loyal niggas that don't mind movin' down here. Do you know some niggas like that?"

P. Diamonds nodded his head. "How many do you need, 'cause I know a lot of hungry killas?"

"Bring in however many you want, but you need to understand that whoever you bring in, they yo' responsibility. So if one violate my family, then you answer to me," Karbonado warned.

That was all P. Diamonds needed to hear. He had a team of niggas that were hungry, and he couldn't wait to put them on.

CHAPTER 24

$$$

Jania was at the house when her parents broke the news to her. "Nia, I can't let you have that party right now," Karbonado told her.

"Daddy, come on. I been waiting on this party for a year!" she complained. "You promised me I could have a party for my 17th birthday." She looked at him with moist eyes.

"I know what I said and shit happens. But let me make it up, Nia. I want to take you to Miami with me. You and yo' girls can come and I promise you will have fun. And next year we'll have a little different circumstances and I'll throw you a big party for yo' 18th birthday."

Jania smiled real big. "Okay, you win, but I better get my big day next year or I won't talk to you until my 19th birthday." He hugged her and then kissed her on the forehead.

"I'm takin' you to Miami next week, so tell yo' lil hoodlum friends to ask their parents. And I want it in writin'." He knew how kids would lie to get their way.

"My friends ain't no hoodlums," she said, laughing. "And you don't have to worry about one of them lying about being able to go. I'll make sure it's really cool."

Karbonado nodded at her and walked out of her room.

Jania didn't want to argue with her parents so she pretended to be okay. But she was really upset because she had looked forward to the party for a long time. She never had one growing up. But she did understand because she knew that the situation with Young Hogg wasn't a joke, and she would never forgive herself if something happened to her family or friends because she insisted on having a party.

What she didn't know was that Karbonado had set up a party for her in Miami and T.I. would be performing. He knew Jania would be very happy once she saw her favorite rapper in person.

*****

Karbonado had just purchased Jania a Bentley coupe for her birthday. He planned on giving it to her when they came back from Miami. Karbonado knew she would love the gift because she had always talked about how she would buy a Bentley coupe with the money she made from her mixtape. He decided he didn't want her to spend her money on a car, even though Checkmate tried to convince him to at least wait until Jania's 18th birthday. He wasn't trying to hear that so she just let him do what he wanted to do.

After signing the paperwork, he left the dealership and went to put some 22" Ashantis on it. Once he finished getting the Bentley tricked out, he went and stashed the car at Damn Fool's house. Upon arriving at his boyz' spot, he decided to stay and kick it a while.

They were in Damn Fool's game room when Karbonado got a call from P. Diamonds. Diamonds explained that he made some calls and eight of his boyz were ready to get money and put in work. Karbonado informed him that he would be in Miami the following week and would meet with them and front them the cash to move to Houston and get themselves set up.

After talking with P. Diamonds, Karbonado and Damn Fool began discussing their plans to take over Texas. While planning it all out, Kiara came into the room and interrupted their conversation. "What's up, baby?" Damn Fool asked.

"I just wanted to see how long you were gonna have company because my mom is about to come by and we are gonna go do some shopping."

"I don't know, but you good. Just bring me something back," he told her and gave her a kiss. Then he continued talking to Karbonado. "Say, bro, you heard of them niggas from 5th ward that's been jackin' all them niggas on the southwest and southside?"

"Yeah, I just hope we don't have to kill none of them wild motherfuckas," Karbonado responded.

"I was thinkin' maybe we could see if they would join our team," Damn Fool suggested.

"Why would you suggest that?" Karbonado asked, looking at Damn Fool crazy.

"Think about it. We could use them to help take over the city. Niggas are already fearin' them. They already jackin' and killin'. So if we add 'em to our team, we just addin' more muscle."

"Yeah, you got a point. We can use them to move on niggas all over Texas."

Karbonado was now planning to try and recruit the young wild boys from 5th ward.

CHAPTER 25

$$$

Karbonado, Checkmate, Jania, and her friends had just arrived in Miami. Diamond Dawg had a limo pick them up, and they would be staying at his four story mansion. Checkmate and the girls had never seen anything so luxurious. Karbonado admired how Diamond Dawg was living and knew he needed to step up his game.

"Baby, this motherfucka is off the chain!" Checkmate said with much excitement.

"Yeah, but this isn't shit. The house he live in is badder than this one." The house they were staying in was a place that Diamond Dawg owned on Star Island. It was very nice, but not quite as lavish as Diamond Dawg's main residence.

Checkmate was in love with the house. She walked to the middle of the house and was at a loss for words. The mansion had glass windows from floor to ceiling that allowed sight of the extravagant backyard, which was manicured to perfection and contained an oceanfront view to boot. The 15-bedroom abode had marbled floors and an elevator.

Checkmate couldn't even sit down after the trip because she was so in love with the place, and Karbonado had seen the gleam in her eyes.

After an hour of taking in the beauty of the place, the girls settled in, while Karbonado finished up a phone call with Twinkle and Star. They were happy to hear from him again, and Star had chewed his ass out for not calling sooner nor inviting them to Houston like he had promised. But after Karbonado explained everything he had gone through, she was very understanding.

Star told him she was going to come through, and an hour later, she showed up with Twinkle and a friend named Mia. Karbonado tried to control himself by not saying much, but finally, he let it out. "Damn, you finah than a motherfucka!" he said and grabbed her hand.

"Boy, chill yo' perverted ass out!" Star told him, laughing. She had already known he would like Mia, most men and women did. Mia was five foot eight, 150 pounds, with beautiful, smooth, butterscotch skin. She favored Wankaego, and Karbonado was infatuated with her.

"Mia, this my crazy homeboy, Karbonado, and he's off-limits," she said, very serious.

"Damn, Star, you gonna block a nigga shine like that?" he asked. "I try to holla at you and you shoot me down, and now you making Wankaego shoot me down too," he said, frustrated.

Star and Twinkle thought that was so funny they couldn't stop laughing. "Nigga, ain't nobody blockin', I just don't want you messin' with my best friend. Now any other woman out here, you can have and I'll be cool with it, but Mia is off limits."

Karbonado smiled, and said, "Well how 'bout you, since you say anybody else but Mia?" He thought he'd try shootin' his shot again.

The twins laughed again, and he just gave up. They acted like he was some damn circus clown, always laughing at him. "Y'all always

166

think shit funny! Like I'm a clown or somethin'!" Karbonado started laughing because Star wouldn't stop.

By this time, Checkmate came downstairs and Karbonado introduced her to Star, Twinkle, and Mia. The twins gave her a hug and welcomed her to Miami. "I promise you will enjoy every minute you spend in Miami. Anything you want or need, just ask and it's done," Star assured her.

Checkmate immediately took a liking to the twins and couldn't understand why, but she didn't stress it because she knew she was good when it came to judging people's character.

While they were hanging out, Diamond Dawg called Karbonado. "What's up, my mon?" he asked.

"Ah, Diamond, I'm good, just enjoyin' this trip to Miami. When am I gonna see you?"

"I'll have someone pick you up and we can talk about a few things, then I'll take you through the city to meet a few of my people," he promised.

After they hung up, the twins decided they would hit their grandfather's bar. "Are y'all drivin' home drunk?" Karbonado asked.

The twins started laughing. "Nope, we'll stay here. I mean, this is our family's house," Star said.

After that, they got high and drunk on the best shit money could buy. By midnight, Checkmate and Karbonado were wasted. They decided to hit the bed and get some sleep, but to Karbonado's surprise, Checkmate had something else in mind.

"You bet not fuck that bitch," she said with a calm demeanor.

"What bitch?" Karbonado asked, playing dumb. "Why you trippin'?"1

"Look, cut the bullshit. I see how you were lookin' at that girl Mia. You a man and I'm not mad at you because the bitch bad. But if I find

167

out you stickin' yo' dick in that hoe, I'm leavin'. I give you everything and I don't ask for much, but don't play with me and Kaci's feelings." Karbonado was far from stupid. He could see that Checkmate was serious. She really was feeling some type of way about how he was looking at Mia. She wasn't jealous often, but she got that way when she felt he was really feeling some bitch.

"Baby, you my bitch. I don't give a fuck about nobody else. I love you and Kaci. So stop trippin'." He tried to be reassuring by kissing her, and she kissed him back.

"I'm serious, don't make me kill that hoe and leave yo' ass," she said and rolled over and went to sleep.

Karbonado was shocked. She was a little jealous sometimes, but this was different. Checkmate was acting insecure, and he had never seen that in her. After a chill caused the hairs on his arms to rise, he shook it off. Thirty minutes later, he fell asleep with Mia on his mind.

*****

The next morning, Karbonado woke up and got ready to meet with Diamond Dawg. Once he was dressed, he walked to the living room to see where everyone was. Star, Twinkle, and Mia were all passed out. He woke Star up and let her know he was going to meet her grandfather. She got up and hurried to get ready because she wanted to ride with him.

Karbonado really enjoyed Star because she reminded him of Rowdy. She always wanted to kick it and talk shit, plus they got along well. Even though he would flirt with her from time to time, he knew if he fucked her, or even Mia, things may go sour between them. So he decided to never cross that line for the sake of friendship. Plus, he didn't want Checkmate killing nobody.

When they made it to Diamond Dawg's main residence, Star ran in like a kid in a candy store. Diamond Dawg came out to the porch and passed Karbonado a blunt. They sat on the wicker furniture and smoke some very good weed. While they sat and smoked, Karbonado updated Diamond Dawg on everything that had gone on since he had last been to Miami, including adapting Jania and the three kids that had been born recently.

He also explained the beef he had with the Garden City Cartel. Diamond Dawg offered him his hit squad and Karbonado declined. He stated that he had to prove to the streets that he was not to be fucked with, and he needed to capture his father's killer his way. Diamond Dawg respected that, and he knew that Karbonado was just like his father.

They talked for about an hour then Diamond Dawg took them to the slums of Miami so Karbonado could get his face known. Everyone showed Karbonado some love, and Diamond Dawg laid out the red carpet so that he could go anyplace he wanted to go in Miami. Diamond Dawg also gave him a crew to move around with until everyone in the city learned that he was with the man who ran the city. After that, he would be free to move deep without any problems.

CHAPTER 26

$$$

Karbonado had been in Miami for two days and the girls were having the time of their lives. It was going on 10PM, and Karbonado and Checkmate were getting ready to take Jania to Club Prive and surprise her.

Karbonado had on some white Gucci jeans with a red Gucci shirt that had white pin stripes. He also was wearing a red Gucci belt and all red Mauris.

Checkmate wore an all-white Prada dress and red Givenchy pumps. Even the four girls were dressed to impress and looking like money.

"Jania, come here," Karbonado called. When she went to see what he wanted, he gave her a gift wrapped in beautiful silver paper with a white bow. She opened the gift and couldn't believe her father had given her a Rolex flooded with diamonds. It was the same watch she had seen in the jewelry store a year ago.

"Daddy, thank you!" she said excitedly and with a few tears in her eyes. After he put the watch on for her, Checkmate handed her another present. Jania opened the box and smiled at her mother. Checkmate had given her a bracelet that spelled her name with each letter shining in different colored diamonds. "Thank you, Momma!" she said with as much excitement as she felt when she opened the watch. She hugged her mother, doing her best not to cry. She had never gotten such expensive gifts before.

After the gifts were opened, they got ready to leave. As they walked out of the house, Jania noticed that her parents were wearing the same Rolex she had just gotten for her birthday. She just smiled and walked out the door, feeling like the baddest bitch on the planet.

When they pulled up to Club Prive, it was so packed Jania thought they wouldn't get in. She had never been to a club, but because of Diamond Dawg, nobody checked Karbonado's or his crew's IDs. Inside, Jania was wordless. She stood still and got all teary-eyed as she read a banner that said "Happy 17th Birthday Jania". She looked at her parents and they smiled.

"Go, girl, have some fun now and thank me later," Karbonado told her, laughing at the expression on Jania's face.

By this time, she noticed her aunts, Rowdy and Lil Moma, and Kaci all smiling at her. She walked up to them and gave all three women hugs, then went to the dance floor and started enjoying her party. P. Diamond walked out on the floor and grabbed her hand and pulled her to the side.

"What I gotta do to get you to be my wifey?" he asked, joking.

Jania laughed at him. "How you expect me to be your wifey and you didn't get me a present?"

"What make you believe that I didn't get you nothin'?" he questioned, his eyebrows raised suspiciously.

Jania held out her hand. "Well, what are you waiting on?" she asked impatiently.

"I ain't got nothin' right now. It's on layaway."

She couldn't help but laugh. "You silly, boy. Can I at least get a dance for my birthday?" They grabbed each other and began dancing.

After being on the dance floor for over an hour with P. Diamonds and her three friends, she needed a break. "Girl, what you doin'?" her Aunt Rowdy asked.

"I'm tired. I need to take a break."

"Well, you can rest later. Come on!" Rowdy grabbed her hand and pulled her back out on the floor. That was about the time that T.I. walked in and got on the stage.

The whole club, including Jania, went crazy. T.I. performed all of his hits. After he was six songs in, he gave a shout out to the birthday girl. He then walked over to her and gave Jania an autographed copy of his latest album called *Paper Trail*. He capped off her birthday celebration with several pictures of them together.

At the end of the night, Jania was so excited. She kept telling anyone who would listen that she had experienced the best time of her life.

*****

Karbonado, Checkmate, Jania, and her three friends had just gotten off the plane and exited the airport. When they made it to Karbonado's truck, Jania saw a candy blue Bentley coupe and damn near lost her mind.

"Ooooh, Daddy, this car is off the chain! I'm tellin' you I'm gettin' one just like this when I make my bread!" She was yelling she was so excited.

"Girl, quit boppin' and bring yo' ass on!" Checkmate told her.

But Jania wasn't trying to hear it. She started taking pictures of the car then pictures of her with the car. She was the selfie queen.

Karbonado was laughing and encouraging her. "That's what I'm talkin' about. Act like it yours. Face this way...Now that way." He was snapping pictures like a professional photographer snapping shots of a supermodel, all the while laughing at her antics.

"Girl, get yo' ass down! You goin' too far!" Checkmate yelled at her when she started posing on the hood of the car as if she was Tyra Banks or somebody.

Jania jumped down, realizing she had gotten caught up in the moment and was trippin'. "I'm sorry if I was embarassing y'all, but that car is so fine!" she said, serious as a heart attack.

Her friends just laughed and laughed at her and were about to get in the truck until Karbonado handed Jania the keys to the Bentley. When she saw the Bentley symbol on the keychain, she got bug-eyed as she looked at her father. Karbonado just nodded at the car, and she went crazy all over again.

"Oh, my God! Thank you! Thank you! Thank you, Daddy!" She cried and jumped all over her parents, more excited than an old Black woman hit by the Holy Ghost at a Pentecostal revival. She couldn't stop telling them how much she loved them and how happy and grateful she was. She told them at least 20 times how much she appreciated everything they had done for her.

Then she broke down and cried and cried, overwhelmed with joy and love that someone would do so much for her.

After Karbonado and Checkmate hugged her and got Jania calmed down to the point where she was just hiccupping, Checkmate said, "Are you gonna stand here and cry and talk all night, or are you gonna jump in yo' new whip and see how it ride?"

Jania got in her car and told her friends to get in. Before she pulled off, she looked at her best friends and gave them some food for thought. "I just turned 17, and y'all three are 18. How many people you know can say they rode in a Bentley at our age?" she asked. "I say all that to say this: If I shine then y'all shine. So when I pull up to the school house in this sexy motherfucka, we will turn heads and when my music start selling, each one of you will have a sexy car of your pick," she promised each of her friends, and they knew she meant it.

Checkmate had always told her if she shine, it's best that she share her shine with the ones that were around when she had nothing. And that's a lesson that Jania had never forgotten. Whenever she went shopping, she made sure her girls got something.

As she was driving, her phone rang. "Hello," she answered.

"You better enjoy that car, and I hope you can protect yo' self," the caller stated.

"Who is this?" Jania asked, nervous.

"It don't matter, just know you next on my hit list, bitch!" the caller yelled, then hung up.

Jania looked at the phone and sat it down in her lap. She was scared as hell, but she kept her cool because she knew that her parents were right behind her. She knew that whoever the caller was, he was watching them. He had known about the car. She decided not to tell her parents about the call because she didn't want them to keep her from riding through the city. She would just make it a point to step up her own personal security.

And that was a mistake she would learn about later.

CHAPTER 27

$$$

Jania was in the studio puttin' down her verse to a song she wrote when she was interrupted by one of the bodyguards. He gave her a Loui duffle bag that read: Return to Sender. She smiled because she thought P. Diamonds had finally got her the birthday present he had promised her. But when she opened it, she couldn't believe what she was looking at.

Jania began to scream and cry. Big Doe heard her and rushed in to see what was wrong. "Why you screamin', Nia? What's wrong?

She pointed to the bag. "They killed my friends! They killed my friends!" she cried.

Big Doe took a peek in the Loui bag and he couldn't stand the sight of the three heads wrapped in plastic. He read the tag on the bag and knew exactly what it meant. Young Hogg was sending them a message, letting them know that whatever they did, he would do back.

Jania couldn't stop crying. She was hurt because she felt that she didn't protect her friends. She realized too late that she should have taken the threat seriously and told her parents. She didn't and her friends paid the price with their lives.

As she stood there balling, Big Doe called Karbonado and Checkmate. Once they arrived, they tried to calm her down, but Jania couldn't control the anger and hurt that was boiling in her blood. Checkmate told Jania that she would make them pay, but Jania wasn't listening.

Her parents ordered Big Doe to drop Jania off at home, and he did as he was told. When they got there, she went straight to her room and cried herself to sleep.

*****

"I bet that got 'em shook now!" one of The Body Snatchers yelled, excited.

"Listen, y'all calm down. We ain't dealin' with no soft motherfuckas. All we did was piss them off and I guarantee they will try to strike back. So here's the next easy target."

Young Hogg paused. "We need to kill Kaci Conner. That's their precious attorney and Checkmate's girlfriend. She also has a baby by Karbonado," Young Hogg informed them.

"Now, how you know all that, Hogg?" one of The Body Snatchers asked.

"'Cause don't shit go on in my city without me knowin'," Hogg replied.

"Damn, I can't tell. Matter fact, since you know everything that go an in ya city, where do this nigga live? 'Cause we can easily hit him up at his house," one the Body Snatchers said with anger.

Young Hogg didn't respond and that was all The Body Snatchers needed. "Okay, where do we find this Kaci Conner bitch?" one of them asked.

Young Hogg said, "She work in the courthouse everyday." He took out a picture and passed it around. "All you got to do is snatch her up before she get into her car tomorrow," he told them.

"Okay, we got her. But if you knew this, why the hell you didn't off the bitch already?" one of them asked, curious.

"Because I left town to duck my family off. I know when I strike, they're gonna strike back and I refuse to let them touch my family again," he explained, the pain still evident on his face.

The Body Snatcher realized he was still grieving. "Look, Hogg, we gonna get them motherfuckers. Matter fact, we gonna make Kaci Conner give us everything we need to know about Black Diamond Cartel," they promised Young Hogg, and he knew they wouldn't let him down.

*****

Jania was awake and looking at old pictures of her and her friends. She couldn't believe they were dead. Every time she thought about them, she got flashbacks about the night she killed Chico.

"You either take responsibility for yo ' actions or you can die with Chico! You are responsible for the people you bring around, just like everybody else in our family." Her mother's words continued to echo in her mind.

Jania got up from her bed and walked downstairs to her parents' room. She knocked on their door and walked in after her mother gave her the okay. "What's up, Nia?" Checkmate asked.

Jania walked over to their bed and sat down on the side. "Momma, I can't let those niggas get away with killin' my friends," she stated then began crying again.

Checkmate took her daughter into her arms, knowing that only time would heal her wounds, and even then, some of them would always be there. "It's okay, Nia. Let it out. I'm gonna make them pay, baby. I promise."

"No, Momma," Jania said, pulling away from Checkmate. "I'm going to make them pay!" Checkmate knew Jania was angry and hurt, but she couldn't believe how her daughter was talking. "I'm gonna kill them bitch ass niggas. They killed my friends for no reason! I brought them around, and now they're dead because I didn't protect them!" Jania yelled and cried, shocking her parents by the things she said. It was rare that she got salty with her language, especially considering she was in the rap game. But right now, there was no filter over her mouth, she was simply saying what she felt.

Checkmate understood because she had damn near lost her mind when they tried to kill Karbonado. "Okay, Nia. But if you gonna play this game, you gotta play it right," she warned.

"That's the problem, y'all playing games with this nigga and he's not!" she screamed and left the room.

Checkmate was stunned by her attitude, and that's when she realized one thing: her daughter was no longer the sweet, innocent Jania.

Young Hogg had just created a monster.

*****

"Girl, why are you blowing my phone up?" Kaci asked Kiara.

Kiara had been at home by herself for two days and she was bored. She wanted someone to talk to so she called her best friend. "Damn, you been acting really funny. I guess since you got a man and a woman, it's fuck Keke now?" Kiara said, mad.

Kaci started laughing because she knew it was the pregnancy making her so sensitive. "Girl, you know I love you and ain't nothin' or nobody gonna change that," she said, serious.

"Yeah, that's what ya mouth says, but you ain't been showing me that." She pouted.

"Kiara, you trippin'. How about tomorrow I take you to lunch?"

"Okay, but I'm still mad 'cause you haven't called me all day yesterday or today," Kiara said like a spoiled child.

"Girl, bye. I'll come pick you up tomorrow." She laughed and hung up the phone.

Kaci was walking to her car and was caught off guard when a man with a mask on jumped out at her. She screamed and turned around in an attempt to run, but was surprised by another masked man behind her holding a .45 semi-automatic pistol.

"Bitch, if you want to live, I suggest you shut the fuck up!"

Kaci was more scared than she had ever been in her life, and all she could think about was her daughter and son. She walked with the two Body Snatchers when suddenly she heard two gunshots.

She looked on both sides of her and saw both of the masked men lying on the ground with holes in their heads. "Kaci, let's go!" she heard someone say and grab her hand, rushing to her car.

When she got to her vehicle, she jumped in the driver's seat, and her passenger got in on the passenger's side. She looked at him, and all she could do was say thank you.

"Fuck all that, Kaci. Let's go. It's two dead motherfuckas over there!" her savior told her. She drove off and jumped on the freeway.

Ten minutes later, the man who saved her life received a phone call. "Yo, what's up?...Yeah, I got her...Yeah, okay." He hung up. Kaci began to get nervous again, and he told her, "Calm down. I'm not here to hurt you. Karbonado sent me to make sure you made it home."

"What is your name?" she asked, as if it made a difference.

"They call me Trigga Man," he told her while he scrolled through his phone. After he pushed send, he waited on the other person to answer.

"Hello," Karbonado said, and Trigga Man handed Kaci the phone.

When she heard Karbonado's voice, everything that happened became real and she was flooded with emotion. "Baby," she said, crying, "I'm so glad to hear your voice. I was so scared, they tried to kill me!"

"Hey, calm down, you're safe now. We will talk when you get home," he told her and she hung up.

"Thank you," she told Trigga Man, feeling a little better.

"It's all good, just make sure you keep me out of jail," he said, quite serious.

"I got you. I owe you for saving my life. I'm forever in debt to you," she promised, and that was all he said.

Karbonado was about to send him on a murder spree and he just might need some legal help in the near future.

CHAPTER 28

$$$

The last two weeks had been a bloody mess. Young Hogg had five of Karbonado's spots shut down, and Karbonado had killed at least ten of Young Hogg's souljas.

The city of Houston was so hot, J-Money had called a meeting with Karbonado. "You have to end this war, kinfolk. The feds are about to get involved, and I am not in their league. I can't protect you from them if they get involved," J-Money warned.

"Man, fuck the feds. This bitch ass nigga killed my pops, then he laid a few of my boys out. Worst of all, he killed three innocent girls, friends of my daughter, and put their heads in a bag. Fuck Young Hogg, fuck the feds, and fuck you if you ain't down! It's kill or be killed!" Karbonado shouted with anger.

"Look, Karbonado, we supposed to be gettin' money. We can't do that if you got the streets hot! I'm not sayin' let them niggas make it. All I'm sayin' is you need to hurry and end this shit." J-Money understood the realities of the streets, about not lettin' nobody handle you, but he was tryin' to get his paper.

"I been tryin' to find this nigga, but it's been no luck. We gotta get to his family. Checkmate smoked his brother and sister, but this nigga still think we playin'!"

J-Money pulled an envelope out of his jacket pocket and handed it to Karbonado. "Here's his grandmother address. She live in Kenner, Louisiana. You should pay her a visit and see how he handle that. But I'm tellin' you, you gotta hurry and end this," J-Money told him with a straight face.

Karbonado looked at the information and smiled because he knew that he would be able to get Young Hogg out of his hiding place now.

He called Checkmate. "What's up, baby?" she asked.

"Baby, I got that nigga info. Pack some clothes 'cause we about to take a trip. We not gonna send nobody else. We gonna take care of this ourselves," he said excitedly.

"Okay, I'll be ready when you get here," Checkmate told him and hung up.

Twenty minutes later, Karbonado walked through the front door, shocked to see Jania sitting on the couch, holding a 9mm in her lap. "Nia, what the hell do you think you doin'?!"

"I'm doin' what I should be doin'. I'm about to start revengin' my dead friends," she said with a straight face.

Karbonado started laughing, but it wasn't a funny laugh. "Girl, I don't got time to play with you. Now put that gun up," he told her and walked to his bedroom. Jania just sat there, ignoring her father's order. Karbonado entered the bedroom and Checkmate was just closing her bag. "Baby," he said, "We goin' to the Boot. I got Young Hogg grandmother address. I got a good idea, so let's hit the road."

"Okay, but we takin' Nia with us," she informed him.

"You trippin' and she trippin'. Baby, that's not a good idea. We goin' on a serious mission and I don't have time to do no babysittin'. "

"Baby, you may not have noticed the last couple a weeks, but Nia is not the same. She want her revenge, and we would too if it was us, so I'm about to give her that chance. She been workin' with that heat she carryin' around, and she can take it apart, put it together, and shoot it like she always been doin' it. So my mind made up, she goin'. If she get out there and bitch up, I'll never bring her on another mission again. But I see it in her eyes. She serious. And if you be real, you see it too."

"A'ight, fuck it, let's go. Is Kaci good with the kids?"

"Hell, yeah. She safe and I got a serious team of killas surroundin' our house. A nigga won't make it to our doorstep without gettin' ambushed," she said with confidence.

"Okay, then let's ride out," Karbonado said, grabbing his keys and walking out the door. In the car, he called P. Diamonds and told him to meet him at one of the trap houses. He ordered him to bring two of his men with him.

*****

Checkmate, Karbonado, Jania, P. Diamonds, and two of his men made it to Louisiana with no problems. They parked down the street from Young Hogg's grandmother's place. Karbonado had gone over the plan several times while he was driving, and everybody was ready to roll.

"Baby, you stay in the car and watch the street," Karbonado ordered.

"Okay, but hurry up," Checkmate replied.

He got out of the car, then signaled for P. Diamonds and his two boys to exit their car, too. When they got to the front door, one of P. Diamonds crew kicked it wide open.

All four men rushed inside the house with masked faces and forced Young Hogg's wife and kids on the floor. When Young Hogg's wife began to scream, P. Diamonds slapped her across the head with his pistol.

"Bitch, close yo' mouth befo' I open yo' brains!" He warned her loudly. Young Hogg's wife was so frightened, she pissed on herself.

Karbonado and one of the other men had already moved to the back room to make sure Hogg hadn't left any goons behind. When they returned, Karbonado was leading Young Hogg's grandmother.

Misunderstanding why these armed and masked men had broken into her home, she said, "Chile, whatever it is y'all want, I don't have much, but y'all can have it all."

Karbonado replied, "I want Young Hogg. Now if you give him up, y'all will live. But if you play games I'll kill everyone of y'all. Now come on!" He took them to the truck.

Karbonado drove them to his father's friend who went by the name Gator who lived right next to the swamp and had four gators that he used to feed Trap Money's enemies. When they made it to Gator's spot, he exited the truck and he and the crew went to talk to his pop's friend.

"What's up, neph?" Gator asked when he answered the door. "What you bring my boys to eat?" Gator always got straight to business. When he smiled, he looked like the backwoods, swamp nigga he was, half his teeth missing.

Karbonado looked at P. Diamonds, and said, "Get 'em." P. Diamonds and his crew did what they were told, and brought Young Hogg's family out of the car. Gator led the whole gang to the swamp.

"Please, don't kill us. Please!" Young Hogg's wife and grandmother begged for the family's lives.

"I'll tell you what," Karbonado told them, "if you can convince my little girl to let you live, then I'll let you live." He looked at Jania.

"Baby, please, we have nothin' to do with whatever Young Hogg did to you and yo' father," the grandmother pleaded. "Please don't let us die." The old woman was crying and she hoped her tears would mean something to Jania.

Jania walked over to the woman with tears in her eyes. She pulled out her cellphone and showed Young Hogg's grandmother a picture of her three friends. "These were my best friends. They were just like y'all! They had nothing to do with my father and Young Hogg. But did that stop him from chopping their heads off? No! He didn't give a fuck, and now I must be the same way."

Jania pulled her nine out and shot Young Hogg's grandmother in the face.

Checkmate jumped because she was caught off guard. She had expected at least some hesitation from her daughter. Karbonado was even more shocked. He hadn't believed that Jania would do it at all. This showed had much he hadn't paid attention since her friends had died. Not only had the whole thing changed her in a way that was irreversible, but Young Hogg had unleashed the beast within.

She was just about to shoot Young Hogg's wife in the face as well, but Karbonado stopped her. "Hold on, Nia." He pulled out a throw away and pushed the record button. He began recording P. Diamonds as he pushed Young Hogg's grandmother onto the edge of the swamp.

"You see this, bitch ass nigga?!" he yelled, then pushed the old woman into the swamp. He made sure that Hogg knew it was his grandmother, careful to get a closeup of her face, hoping that Young Hogg would lose his mind as the gators ripped her body apart.

Karbonado turned the camera towards Young Hogg's wife and children. "You either give me yo' life, or I'll take theirs!" he shouted with anger.

After ending the video, Karbonado pushed play to make sure he had gotten a good view. Once he was satisfied, he smiled and pushed the send button to the number Hogg's wife had given him. He waited on Young Hogg to make contact with him.

CHAPTER 29

$$$

"Please! Come on, man, don't kill me!" Lil Bobby screamed in pain.

"Listen, lil nigga, all I want is Karbonado and that bitch! If you give 'em up, then I'll let you live. But you will have to leave Texas and never return," Young Hogg told Lil Bobby.

While Young Hogg waited on Bobby to break weak, his phone started ringing, the tone letting him know it was a video text. He was going to look at it after he finished his business, but something told him to open the video.

"Noo! Noo ! Noo!" he yelled. "Fuck! This nigga just killed my grandmother and now he's got my wife and kids," he cried out. Young Hogg couldn't take it. He loved his family so much, he was willing to sacrifice his life for theirs.

He called the number that Karbonado left and told him that he would trade his life for his family.

"Okay, listen, bitch nigga, call yo boyz off and turn yo'self in. If you don't, then they die. I got three hungry gators waitin' to eat," Karbonado warned him. "And this time, I won't shoot them first."

"Okay, man, give me a hour to call my boyz off and I'll meet with you. Just don't kill no more of my family," he begged.

"You got one hour to hit me back, and you better hurry and bring yo' ass. If you think I'm playin', try me," Karbonado shouted and hung up.

Karbonado looked at the group with him and said, "Got that motherfucka now. He not so tough is he?" He laughed that crazy laugh of his.

*****

Young Hogg had just finished talking to Karbonado and was about to send out the order for his boyz to pull up when he received another call.

"Daddy! Daddy!" Lil David said in a panic.

"Lil David, where you at?" Hogg asked his son.

"Daddy, somebody came in and took Big Momma, my momma, and the girls!" he shouted.

"Where are you at?!" Young Hogg asked again.

"I'm still at the house. When they came in, I hid in the closet. Nobody but Granny and Momma know I'm here," Lil David informed his father.

"Okay, listen. I'm goin' to send someone to came scoop you up. Just stay there until I can get you back to the city."

"Okay, I love you, Daddy," Lil David expressed.

"I love you, too, boy!" Young Hogg's soul was crushed. He knew that he would never see his son again. "Damn, I should of protected my family," he said with regret.

Young Hogg knew he had no time to feel sorry about the mistakes he had made, which began with killing Trap Money and ended with not letting it go when the Black Diamond Cartel got even. But it was too late for all that. He had to hurry and place calls to his crew and tell them to fall back.

When the calls were done, he was sure that everyone in his crew had obeyed his orders. He had explained to them that he had to give his life to Karbonado so that his family could survive. Everyone understood and promised to make sure his family would be looked out for.

Young Hogg then put his best friend, Boss in charge of the Garden City Cartel. "Say, Hogg, I promise once we get ya' family back safe, I'm gonna make sure that nigga pay!" Boss told his friend.

Young Hogg walked up to his friend and gave him a hug. "We been through everything together, fam. I can't remember a time you made a promise and didn't keep it. So I know you will handle them niggas. I love you, man," Young Hogg said with tears in his eyes.

Boss was hurt to know he was about to lose his childhood friend. He wanted to go with Young Hogg and fight it out, but he knew Young Hogg wanted to save his family.

After he finished giving instructions, Young Hogg left his boyz and headed to Louisiana with one thing on his mind:

Saving his family.

*****

"Damn, when is this pussy nigga gonna show up?!" P. Diamonds asked, frustrated.

Him and his boyz were sent to meet Young Hogg at a vacant house. They were ordered to tie him up and bring him back to Gator's spot once he arrived.

After waiting on Hogg for six hours, P. Diamonds was relieved to see him pull up. P. Diamonds tied his hands behind his back with zip ties then secured his feet. Once P. Diamonds was sure Young Hogg wasn't going to be get loose, he placed the leader of the Garden City Cartel in the trunk of the car and took him straight to Gator's spot, careful not to draw attention to himself in any way.

Upon arriving, P. Diamonds pulled Young Hogg from the trunk and directed him to Karbonado's location. When Young Hogg saw his family, he lost his temper.

"Let them go, we had a deal!" Young Hogg yelled.

Karbonado smiled. "Damn, I can't lie, you a gangsta fo' real! Even after we showed you our murder game, you still talkin like you runnin' shit!" Karbonado told him.

"Come on, man. You gave me yo' word. If I come, then you let my family live." Hogg had tears of anger in his eyes.

Karbonado thought about what he said and he had to admit that he did say that. "Yeah, I did say that, and I'm a man of my word," he said, then looked at Jania and smiled. "Take care of yo' bizness," he told her.

Jania walked over to Young Hogg's wife and was getting ready to shoot her in the head, but she paused. "P. Diamonds, hand me those ties. Matter fact, just tie her hands to this pole."

The pole was attached to the dock that sat over the swamp. P. Diamonds grabbed Young Hogg's wife, who fought and kicked and screamed, and carried her to the pole, where he zip tied her hands in place. Everybody looked at Jania, wondering what she had in mind.

"P. Diamonds, get me that machete over there." She pointed to the wicked looking cutting tool, and P. Diamonds did what he was told. "Now, here's what I'm gonna do. You killed my girls, so instead of me killin' yo' wife fast, I'm gonna do it nice and slow!" she said. Her anger was so visible that they all took a step back.

"P. Diamonds, every part you cut off, throw it to the gators," Jania directed. Young Hogg went crazy and his wife started bucking as she tried to get away from P. Diamonds. Young Hogg said, "Bitch, you lost yo' fuckin' mind! Untie my wife now!"

"Bitch?" Jania asked, looking at him with murder in her eyes. "Oh, I got yo' bitch. P. Diamonds, chop off her legs, but first put a tourniquet around them to slow down the bleedin'."

P. Diamonds signaled one of his boyz, and together, they put zip ties around the tops of her thighs and pulled them as tight as they could get them. Satisfied with the job, P. Diamonds pretended to be Derek Jeter and took a swing with the machete, slicing through bone and tissue like butter.

Young Hogg's wife looked at her leg lying on the ground several feet away before the excruciating pain signal was received by her brain. She screamed so loud that Checkmate had to cover her ears. Blood flew in every direction, some splattering on Jania's cheek. She swiped it away with her forearm then walked over and kicked the leg into the swamp, where the gators wasted no time fighting over the meat.

Checkmate said nothing to this point, allowing Jania to handle this how she saw fit. But now she spoke up. "Nia, we can't keep lettin' her holla like that. Somebody might hear her and call the laws!" she said, worried for them and for Jania's psyche when this was all over.

"Oh, we good. Nobody will hear her 'cause we too far out. Trust me, I've heard worse," Gator informed her.

Jania ignored Checkmate, set on her bloodlust, and told P. Diamonds to untie the woman. P. Diamonds cut her hands free and she hit the deck and dropped, unable to balance herself on one leg.

"Now throw her in the swamp alive," Jania ordered. Young Hogg, who had been whimpering with his eyes closed, once again looked at his wife and screamed as the gators ripped her body piece by piece.

"Don't cry now, bitch nigga. You wasn't cryin' when you killed my friends, so man up!" Jania yelled at him.

She turned to P. Diamonds again. "P. Diamonds, put some tape over his mouth so I don't have to listen to that lil bitch." Once P. Diamonds slapped a thick piece of duct tape over Young Hogg's mouth, she said, "I want you to chop both of his kids' heads off, then throw 'em in the swamp." The kids were in absolute shock. They had said nothing since the killing began, only crying as they saw the savagery. Young Hogg, though, even with the tape over his mouth started hissing and bucking and blowing snot bubbles out of his nose. But it did no good. Even though she could make out most of the curse words he spewed from behind the tape, Jania ignored the profanity dictionary, set on her job.

P. Diamonds chopped the heads off and blood flew around like it was a war zone. He tossed them to the gators, the bodies following.

Young Hogg fell to his knees, a crying mess. Jania looked into his eyes without a drop of sympathy and kissed him on the lips. "I'll see you in hell, motherfucka!" she yelled, then emptied her clip.

After she was out of bullets, P. Diamonds pulled Young Hogg's body into the swamp and let the gators destroy the evidence.

Jania walked off the dock and looked at the sky. "I told y'all I was gonna get his bitch ass. Watch over me and protect me. Also, kiss my Granny for me and tell her I love her," she said, her face coated with tears.

Karbonado and Checkmate looked at each other with the same thought: Jania was no longer the same sweet girl. Young Hogg killing her friends had turned her soul stone cold.

CHAPTER 30

$$$

Five Years Later

"Nigga, have you lost yo' fuckin' mind?" Checkmate yelled at Lil Daddy for pushing his sister, Princess, off the slide.

"But, Momma, she called me a crybaby!" he told her.

"No I didn't, Momma. He lyin'!" Princess argued.

"What have I told y'all about fightin' each other?"

"You said that family don't fight each other, we fight our enemies," Lil Daddy and Princess both repeated.

"Then why are y'all fightin'? Do I need to beat both of you until you learn not to fight each other?"

"Nooo, Momma! We sorry, we won't fight no more," they told her as they ran to hug her.

Kaci just laughed and shook her head because she knew Princess and Lil Daddy would be back to fighting in no time. That's how it had been since they were old enough to fight. Princess loved her brother, and he her, but they were just like Checkmate and Karbonado. Most of the time Checkmate ignored their fights, as did Kaci, until they got physical.

Diamond, on the other hand, was quiet and very laid back. She and Asia were always together. Diamond was a real daddy's girl and even though Asia was not her biological sister, couldn't no one tell her different.

Both of them loved Karbonado to death. Anytime he wasn't around to defend himself, nobody could tell them anything bad about him. To Diamond and Asia, he could do no wrong.

"Momma, can I call Daddy?" Lil Daddy asked Kaci. She gave him her phone and allowed him to call his father. Once Karbonado was on the line, he said, "Daddy, can you buy me a new train set?" Apparently his father had said yes because he got so excited, he gave his mother the phone and ran off to tell his sister.

Kaci looked at the phone and noticed that her son had not hung up. "Hey, baby!" Kaci said with joy. She talked with Karbonado for ten minutes then let Checkmate speak to him.

After Checkmate finished her conversation with Karbonado, she watched the kids play and have fun. "Girl," Kaci told her, "our kids are spoiled as hell!"

"Yeah, I know. Look at 'em." Checkmate said, pointing at them. "They're so happy. They have no worries. All they want to do is play and have fun. I pray they continue to live life happy and worry free. I never had two percent of what they got." A tear ran down her face.

"Girl, our kids will never have to grow up the way you did. They will never have to go through none of the shit you went through as a child." Kaci gave her a very intimate hug.

While they were sharing a hug, Checkmate's phone started ringing. "What's up?" she answered. It was Nia and immediately Checkmate started in on her. "We at the park. Where in the hell you been? I been waitin' to hear from you for two days!"

Jania started laughing. "Momma, calm down! I been busy. What time you comin' home?"

"In about an hour. Why?"

"Because I haven't seen you in two days! I miss you and I got something I want to tell you."

"Okay," Checkmate told her, "I'll be home soon, then you can tell me all about it." She hung up. "This bitch lost her mind," she said to Kaci.

"What she do?" Kaci asked.

"The bitch don't call me for two days, then call me now talkin' 'bout she miss me!" Checkmate said, smiling.

"Girl, you know damn well she love you."

"That's not the point. She hadn't called to make sure I'm alive!" Checkmate fussed.

She got up from the bench and decided it was time to gather up the kids and head back to the house. She was curious about what Jania wanted to tell her.

"I hope she ain't made me somebody grandma," she said to herself.

*****

"Damn, Momma, you gettin' fat!" Jania told Checkmate after playfully slapping her on the ass.

"Bitch, yo' daddy love it. So that's all that matter to me! And well, Kaci love it, too." Checkmate laughed. She had put on a little weight in her breasts and ass. "Why yo' ass ain't been by here? What, P. Diamonds keeping you locked in the house?" she asked, fussing again because she missed her daughter.

"Aww, you jealous?" Jania said before answering her question. When Checkmate just looked at her, Jania continued, "Me and P. went to Miami. He wanted to show me around and introduce me to his sister, Five Star. We all went to a Miami Heat game, and he proposed to me at halftime," Jania said, suddenly excited as she showed her mother her engagement ring.

Checkmate could not believe her daughter was planning on getting married. At 22, she was old enough, but it was still a surprise. "I'm happy for you, Nia. Just make sure that this is what you really want. If you love him, then make sure you there for him through everything."

"Oh, Momma, that's what I love about you the most. You always support me and that means everything to me." Jania gave her a hug.

"And next time," Checkmate said seriously, "you let me know when you leavin' this city. You may be grown, but I'm still yo momma." Jania laughed, but she understood what Checkmate was saying. It had been five years since all that mess with Young Hogg and the Garden City Cartel, but Checkmate never forgot the viciousness of the game. Old enemies could raise up at any time. She liked to know where Jania was.

Still, Jania made a joke. "Okay, big momma!"

Checkmate jumped up and wrestled Jania down until she screamed. "Okay, I'm sorry, Momma! I'm sorry!" They were both laughing hard.

Checkmate let her up and Jania noticed the tears. "I can't believe you grew up so fast. Just yesterday, you was 15. Now you about to move out and get married." Checkmate looked at her with a sob in her throat. "Don't let nothin' come between yo' family, Jania."

"Momma, you know ain't nothin' comin' between us. I love you, Daddy, my brother and sisters, and even Kaci. So stop worrying. I'll be fine."

*****

196

"Look, all you gotta do is hook the chain to the machine," Bullshit told his friend, Peanut.

Bullshit had snuck off with his mother's boyfriend's truck. He had already planned everything out and now he was about to steal the change machine that sat outside the laundromat.

"Bullshit, how about I drive and let you hook the chain? I don't want to fuck up and not hook it in the right place," Peanut told him.

Bullshit thought about it and understood what his friend meant. He had been drilling him for two days about making sure the chain was connected to the machine just right. Because if he didn't, the machine wouldn't move.

"Alright, I'll hook it and you drive," Bullshit said. He cut off the truck and Peanut slid over into the driver's seat. Peanut backed the truck up and parked right in front of the change machine. He placed the chain around the bumper of the truck and then hooked the other end to the machine.

Bullshit yanked the chain several times to make sure it was set right. After he felt good about the way he had it set, he gave Peanut the signal to hit the gas pedal.

"Okay," Bullshit said, "let's get it as soon as we snatch this bitch up. You gotta jump out and help me put it on the back of the truck." Peanut nodded at the coaching. "Alright, let's go on three... One, two, three!"

Skeeerrr! BAM! was the only thing you could hear.

"Aww, fuck! Damn, nigga, we snatched the whole bumper off!" Bullshit yelled. He knew he was in some shit now, which was normally the case and how he got his name.

"Come on, nigga, we gotta go! I know somebody heard us!" Peanut warned.

"Hold on. We gotta get the bumper."

197

"Nigga, fuck that bumper, let's go!" Peanut yelled, ready to get the hell out of there. Bullshit wanted to get the bumper so bad, but he didn't want to take a chance and get busted. He ran and jumped into the truck with only one thing on his mind.

"How the fuck do I explain this shit?" Bullshit said to himself.

The next morning, Bullshit and Peanut were in the room asleep when Miss Jones came in yelling. "Bullshit!" she screamed, rapping him on his shoulder. "Nigga, what the fuck happened to Kerry truck?"

"Momma, what is you talkin' about?" Bullshit asked, trying to play dumb.

"Boy, don't fuckin' play with me! You know damn well what I'm talkin' about! Last night, wasn't shit wrong with his truck and now he get up to go to work and his whole bumper missin'!"

"Momma, for real, I don't know nothin' about that," he said, continuing to deny, deny, deny. "And can you please stop hollerin'?"

"Oh, you think this shit funny, Peanut?" she asked, yelling at her son's friend because she could hear him chuckling under the covers in the extra twin bed in Bullshit's room.

"Momma Jones, I'm not laughin' at you," he told her.

"You know what, Peanut? You and this nigga not gonna be happy until I beat y'all ass! You always runnin' with this nigga and stayin' in some bullshit! Get yo' ass up and get out my house!"

Peanut did as he was told. He knew Miss Jones was telling the truth. He and Bullshit was always in some bullshit. He walked out of the door and began to laugh for real, thinking about the mess they got into the night before.

"Why she actin' surprised? She nicknamed him Bullshit," Peanut said to himself, laughing hard.

CHAPTER 31

$$$

P. Diamonds was on his way to Cloverland Park to meet one of his customers. He decided to stop at the Burger King on Cullen to grab him something to eat. While he was getting out of the car, a young kid around 15 years old approached him.

"Look out, homie, can you spare me somethin' so I can grab me somethin' to eat?" Peanut asked.

P. Diamonds looked him up and down. He shook his head at the sight of what Peanut had on. Peanut never had much because his sister could barely afford much. P. Diamonds reached into his pocket and pulled out a knot of money. Peanut's eyes grew big as golf balls as he watched P. Diamonds peel off two hundred-dollar bills and hand them to him.

"Lil nigga, get you somethin' to eat and go to that shoe store in the parkin' lot of Fiesta and get you a fresh pair of Forces or Air Max," P. Diamonds told him then walked into the Burger King.

After P. Diamonds ordered his food, he left and went to Cloverland to meet Duck. Duck got out of his car when he saw P. Diamonds pull up behind him. P. Diamonds exited his vehicle, gave Duck a pound of dro out of his trunk, then left in a hurry so he could pick up Jania from the studio.

While he was riding down Cullen, headed towards 610 freeway, he noticed Peanut flagging him down in the Fiesta parking lot. P. Diamonds pulled over and Peanut ran across the street and got in the car.

"Lil homie, where you think you goin'?" P. Diamonds asked.

"You headin' that way. Can you drop me off? I live in Westley Square," Peanut told him.

P. Diamonds shook his head and laughed. "I guess you ain't givin' me a choice." He pulled out, rolling towards Westley Square. While driving, he listened to Jania's last single called "Checkmate."

"Man, that song jammin'. Is that Starburst?" Peanut asked.

"Yeah, this her newest single. It's not out yet though," he said, smiling.

"She been on fire the past six months," Peanut told him. P. Diamonds nodded his head. He had finally made it to Peanut's crib, but before he let Peanut get out, he wanted to see what he bought from the shoe store.

Peanut pulled out some red and white Air Force Ones. Then he pulled out another pair of the exact same shoes, but a different size.

"Who are the other pair for?" P. Diamonds asked.

"My big sister, April," Peanut said with a smile. P. Diamonds could tell from that smile that he really loved his sister.

"That's what's up."

"I appreciate the money. Nobody ever gave me or my sister shit. Either I'm tryna get it in the streets or my sister bustin' her ass at Fiesta just to have a lil somethin'," Peanut said with his head down.

200

"Where's yo' parents?"

"They died in a car crash. Four years ago." Peanut got a little misty-eyed but didn't let a tear fall. "It's just me and my sis. We all we got."

P. Diamonds felt bad for Peanut. He understood how it felt to not have money. His parents were from Haiti, and he grew up in Miami not having much until he got it from the streets.

"How old are you?" he asked Peanut.

"I'm 15."

P. Diamonds reached into his glovebox and grabbed a pen and a piece of paper. He wrote down his number and handed it to Peanut. "Call me tomorrow at 12PM. I'll come scoop you up and show you how to get some real money. A man supposed to keep a bank roll and food on the table, and also keep his wardrobe up. If you listen to me and soak up everything I show you, you will be rich before you 18," P. Diamonds promised him.

"Thanks again, big2 homie," Peanut told him and got out of the car.

CHAPTER 32

$$$

Three Months Later

P. Diamonds had spent the past three months showing Peanut everything he needed to know about drugs. It didn't take long for Peanut to learn, and that's what P. Diamonds liked the most.

After the first month, he gave Peanut a test and allowed him to run one of his trap houses. The boy did good, never taking any shorts.

One day, Peanut said, "P., I got a homeboy name Bullshit. Can I put him in the trap with me?"

P. Diamonds looked at Peanut like he was crazy. "What's his name again?"

"Bullshit," Peanut said again.

"Nigga, do you think I want a nigga with the title Bullshit around my shit?" he asked, pissed.

Peanut started laughing at the situation and P. Diamonds began to think maybe he was playing a joke.

"Man, I ain't got time for that bullshit, Peanut," P. Diamonds said, laughing.

"For real, P. I know it sound crazy. But that's my boy. His momma nicknamed him that. She say 'cause he always either in some bullshit, on some bullshit, or doin' some bullshit," Peanut explained.

That made P. start laughing again. "Look, I'll let you bring him. But if he fuck up, I'm cuttin' both of you off," P. told him and he was serious. But that was all that Peanut needed to hear. He was puttin' his boy on.

That had been two months ago, and now P. had two young, hungry niggas on his team.

It was time for the Black Diamond Cartel monthly meeting, and P. Diamonds took Peanut and Bullshit to meet the rest of the team.

"Lil Moma, Rowdy, Checkmate, this my two lil niggas I was tellin' y'all about. This Peanut and this Bullshit," P. Diamonds introduced.

"Niggas say they 'bout that drama, well I say I'm 'bout that bullshit!" Bullshit blurted out, causing everybody to laugh.

P. Diamonds told them, "My nigga wild, but he good people. That's Peanut right hand man, and I believe in them lil niggas."

"I like Bullshit," Karbonado told him. "I can see him bein' a boss nigga. Just keep groomin' him and Peanut. I trust yo' judgment."

*****

"You see ol' girl right there?" Boss asked, painting at Checkmate.

"Yeah, that ho' bad!" Dirty shouted.

"Don't let the beauty fool you. That bitch is ruthless. She will not hesitate to kill you. Matter fact, she the one killed yo' uncle and auntie."

Dirty was Young Hogg's son, Lil David. Boss had taken him and groomed him well. For the past five years, they had been watching the Black Diamond Cartel. They were both planning to revenge Young

203

Hogg's death. But Boss wanted to wait and allow them time to forget about the past. The way they had been moving, the Black Diamond Cartel truly thought they ran Houston as they saw fit. It seemed as though the Garden City Cartel was a distant memory.

"We wait another month and we start killin' 'em. The first niggas that gotta go is their hit man, that nigga they call Trigga Man. We can't get to none of them without gettin' him and the rest of their goons out the way," Boss told Dirty.

"You know where they live, why not hit up there?" Dirty asked.

"Because they have too much security. If we make it through the gate, then we may never make it out the gate."

"That's what we got pawns for. Them niggas got all that protection, but I'm not convinced. I say we send our pawns on a run and test that bullshit. We just might get lucky."

Boss didn't think it was a good idea, but he figured he would listen to Dirty—at least he would pretend to listen to Dirty. He already knew what the outcome would be. But he decided to let Dirty see for himself.

"Okay, we put some goons together and tomorrow night we hit 'em up. If you accomplish the mission, then you continue to run the show. But if you fail, you sit back and continue to let me call the shots." Boss began to drive back to the crib with Dirty in the passenger seat putting together a plan to take out the head of the Black Diamond Cartel.

CHAPTER 33

$$$

"Look, y'all gotta jump the gate. That's the only way you will get in there," Dirty told his goons through the earpieces he had gotten them to communicate.

"We got it," one of the goons said. "All you gotta do is make sure once we get in. The rest of the team good."

"Tim already on standby. Just do what we planned!" Dirty snarled into the lapel mic he was wearing.

John John hopped over the fence and was already headed for the house. "Man, this shit sweet. Ain't no guards nowhere. That's alright, I'm 'bout to wreck shop."

By the time John John made it to the front of the house, he had ten of his boyz standing with him and they were ready to cause hell to come visit Karbonado and his family.

John Dahn gazed at his boyz and smiled. "These niggas don't get a chance."

*****

Karbonado and Checkmate woke up to the alarm going off. They looked at the console that was on a table next to their bed and couldn't believe what they observed. There were several heavily armed men on their property.

Checkmate looked at Karbonado and the first thing that came to both of their minds were their kids. They both jumped up, woke Kaci up, and quickly got dressed. They each ran to one of the kids' bedrooms and collected a child. Once the group was gathered up, they proceeded to a secret door that took them to the basement.

"Kaci, take the kids and go all the way down that hall until you see another door. That door leads to another house nobody know about. When you get there call P. and tell him I'm in danger. Don't leave that house until you hear from me." Karbonado kissed her on the cheek and pushed her forward without another word or argument from Kaci. She knew something like this might happen someday and she knew not to waste time arguing with them.

Karbonado slid the secret door closed, and together, he and Checkmate went into war mode.

"These pussies fucked with the wrong nigga," Karbonado said as he loaded his AR15.

While he was getting ready to put in work with the assault rifle, Checkmate pepped up with a Tommy gun.

"Where the fuck you get that!" Karbonado asked. They had been living together for a long time now and he had never seen the gun.

"Cut my stash. Let's go, it's ride or die," she responded, then walked towards the front of the house where the trouble was. *That's my Checkmate*, Karbonado thought as he smiled. She had never been the kind of woman to run from trouble or avoid it.

When the shit came, she got right to it.

Karbonado still had the security tablet and could see where all of his opponents were.

Checkmate wasted no more time.

She shot through the front door and took out three members of the Garden City Cartel, while Karbonado eliminated four more. The other three members were shocked and began scrambling out of the way.

Just when Karbonado and Checkmate thought they might have gotten the upper hand, several more men appeared out of the darkness. They didn't know it, but Dirty sent reinforcements once he heard the shots.

"Fuck!" Checkmate yelled, "it's too many of 'em!"

Checkmate kept squeezing the trigger on the Tommy gun.

The whole time they were at war, all Karbonado could think about was where the fuck his goons were. He was fighting to live, and he vowed to kill every motherfucka that was supposed to be guarding his spot.

"Baby, I'm out!" Checkmate began to panic. She didn't want to leave Karbonado fighting by himself, but she knew she needed some more fire power.

Checkmate ran to grab another weapon. When she made it back, she noticed that there was blood on the floor, and that told her one thing: Karbonado had been shot.

He was still pulling the trigger on the AR-15 and airin' out some of them boyz from Garden City. She stepped beside him, and Karbonado looked down to see that Checkmate had a grenade launcher in her hands.

"Girl, is you crazy? Where the fuck did you get that!"

"Move!" she yelled, then pulled the trigger mechanism on the grenade launcher, blowing the whole front yard into chunks and pieces.

The concussive force was strong enough to knock both of them off their feet, but that wasn't the worst of the damage. Checkmate killed seven people at one time with the blast.

The rest tried running, then she let off several more grenades from the launcher.

When the smoke cleared, they saw that P. Diamonds had arrived on the scene with a clique of goons, and they entered the war. After ten minutes, P. Diamonds and his boyz, along with Karbonado and Checkmate, had killed everybody that had stepped onto their turf.

Karbonado had been shot in the shoulder, but the wound wasn't bad, the bleeding down to a minimum. He had certainly been in worse conditions before, and all he was concerned about was one thing. "Where's them motherfuckas that we pay to watch our home?!" he asked, ready to do some more killin'.

"Dead," P. Diamonds said simply. "They were already dead when we got here."

"Fuck!" Karbonado said, then looked at Checkmate. "And where the fuck did you get that grenade launcher from? I been livin' with you all this time and you mean to tell me you got bombs in this motherfucka?!"

Checkmate just smiled and blew him a kiss. "That's how square bizness I am. When I die, make sure you put on my stone that I was an army." She walked off, still holding the grenade launcher.

"Nigga," P. said, shaking his head and laughing, "that bitch off the chain!"

Karbonado knew that if it had been any other woman at his side, he would have been dead. And that gave him one more reason to love her more than he already did.

* * * * *

208

"Did you see that shit?" Dirty asked Boss, stunned.

He had sat and watched the whole war on his iPad. Dirty had sent up a drone that flew over the gate onto Karbonado's property. The drone had a camera that allowed them to see everything that had taken place.

"This motherfucka shot a bomb!" Dirty shouted, still not believing what he had seen.

"I told you, that's a dangerous bitch!" Boss yelled at Dirty, mad because he had warned him, and now they had warned the Black Diamond Cartel. "And you just got 20 members of our crew wiped the fuck out because you was too stubborn to play it smart!"

CHAPTER 34

$$$

It had been two hours since the attempt on Karbonado and his family's lives had been made. After making sure the house was clean of weapons, he and Checkmate left and pretended to show up just after the chaos.

Detective Moore and Detective Carter were now on the scene, investigating almost two dozen murders in one spot.

"So who tried to kill y'all this time," Detective Carter asked with a smirk on his face.

"Get the fuck out of my face with that bullshit!" Karbonado shouted in anger.

The detective just laughed before making a threat to arrest them. "This time when we get you, you will die on death row. I hope your kids get to enjoy these next few months, 'cause when we get you, they will end up like every other black bastard." Detective Carter walked off after having his say.

It took everything in Karbonado's power for him to not knock his ass out and that smug look off his face.

*****

On the other side of Houston, Peanut and Bullshit were in the trap gettin' it in. Peanut was seeing so much money he didn't know what to do with it all. His sister April was against him sellin' drugs, but he was bringing in so much money to the house that all she could do was accept the fact that he was doing better than her.

Bullshit had also brought his older brother Ted along. It was now three niggas in the trap, pumping everything from weed to crack to syrup, as well as bars, XOs, Viagra, and even bootleg DVDs and CDs. They were pumping so much shit out of their trap, niggas started calling their spot "The Kash House."

"Say, we gonna be rich in no time," Ted told his little bro, Bullshit.

"Nigga, me and Peanut gonna be rich in no time! You gonna be broke 'cause you ain't been doin' shit but trickin' with them dope fiends."

Bullshit laughed. "Nigga, fuck you! Don't get mad 'cause I'm gettin' mo' pussy than a tampon," Ted told Bullshit.

Ted laughed, too. "Whatever, nigga. For real though. You need to start savin' somethin', bro. Look at me. I'm 15 bands to the good already. I got clothes I can't even pronounce that still got the tags on them. And I'm only 16, bro. You 18 and still stay with momma. I'm not tryna live like that, fam. True story," Bullshit told his brother.

Ted had to admit, he didn't have shit to show for all the hustlin' he had been doing. And in a way, he felt bad that his lil bro had more money than he did. But he knew he couldn't be mad because he had the same opportunity his brother had. He just chose to spend all of his money in one spot.

"Say, they havin' a big game at the gamblin' shack on Cullen later. What y'all gonna do?" Ted asked Peanut and Bullshit.

"Shit, we always down do make a profit. But are them old schools gonna let us in?" Bullshit asked.

"Nigga, I fall in that bitch every weekend. That's where I be meetin' some of them bad bitches that I be with."

"A'ight, cool. We gonna fall in there. Matter fact, The Hash House is closed." Bullshit started closing down the spot.

Later that night, the three of them went to the gambling shack on Cullen. It was packed with big money players and bad women were everywhere. Bullshit wasted no time getting in the crap game.

"I need a fader, not a friend!" he shouted, throwing a hundred on the table.

"Bet, youngsta."

Bullshit shot the dice and he hit seven out the door. "Bet back?" he asked.

"Bet, youngsta."

Bullshit shot the dice again, and this time his point was five. "Bet on the nine and five!" he shouted.

"Bet!" one man shouted, putting up fifty.

"Bet," somebody else stated, adding a hundred.

"Bet," a third man said, placing his ten dollars on the table.

Bullshit put up his money to match the other men, but when he got to the ten dollar bill, he put it in his pocket.

"Hey, man, what you doin'? You ain't hit shit!" the man who put up the ten dollars stated.

"Nigga, how dare you disrespect me? You see me bettin' fifty and hunnuds and you place a ten on this table. It's mine now," Bullshit told him, then rolled the dice.

The man placed his hand on the table and stopped the dice from rolling. "Little nigga, if you don't put my money back on this table, we about to have some serious problems," threatened the man, whose name was Pooh.

"Nigga, fuck you. Pussy, I took that. Do somethin' or get yo' bitch ass hands off them dice and let 'em roll." Bullshit placed his .357 on the table.

Pooh raised his hands up. "You got it, homie. Shoot on." He didn't want any problems as far as gun play, so he tried to leave it alone.

That's until Bullshit rolled the dice and crapped out. "Nobody better not touch my money!" Bullshit said.

"Nigga, I ain't that nigga. I'm gettin' my money!" one of the two men said and took his money. This gave the second man confidence to grab his as well.

Bullshit was so mad he looked at Pooh and let him know how he felt. "Nigga, you owe me a hunnud and fifty dollars! Had you not stopped my roll, I would've had they ass!"

"Look out, homie, you beat me for ten. I ain't givin' you shit else," Pooh told him.

"'A'ight, we will see. Let's go, y'all," Bullshit said to Ted and Peanut.

They both knew it wasn't over with. Bullshit wasn't the type to let shit go easy. Just as they were getting ready to go, Bullshit turned around and pulled his .357 out and shot Pooh in the chest three times.

"Now we even, bitch!" Bullshit said to the dead body lying on the floor then spit on him.

CHAPTER 35

$$$

The next day, word had got around that Bullshit killed Pooh. The police were now looking to arrest him, but nobody knew his real name and that bought him some time.

"Man, why you kill that nigga?" P. Diamonds asked Bullshit.

"Big homie, that nigga cost me a bill fifty. He stopped my roll when he wasn't the fader. Then after I crapped out he wouldn't pay up, so I downed his ass." Bullshit told the story like it wasn't a big deal.

"I got you, lil homie. I gotta holla at our lawyer, Kaci Conner to see if she can beat this shit. Just stay out the streets until I get back with you."

"Alright," Bullshit said, "I got you. Thanks, P. "

P. left The Kash House and called Kaci Conner to give her the run down. She informed him that she would have to see what type of evidence the police had on Bullshit and she would get back with P. in a few days.

*****

Kaci hung up the phone with P. Diamonds. Every time she turned around it was something else with the Black Diamond Cartel. "Damn, these niggas doin' too much. First I gotta handle these murders Karbonado and Checkmate did, and now this nigga Bullshit went out and did some bullshit," she said to herself.

*****

Karbonado had just received a phone call from J-Money asking him to meet at their usual spot. Karbonado figured he was pissed, but he had no control over the situation.

Karbonado walked into the warehouse and J-Money wasted no time speaking his mind. "What the fuck was that, Nado?"

"Man, them niggas tried to kill me and my family!"

"Okay, you defended yo' self and yo' family. By law, you in the right, but the rest of that was some unnecessary shit!" J-Money yelled.

"What the fuck was unnecessary about killin' a motherfucka when they on my property with guns tryna kill my family?!"

"I'm talkin' about the fuckin' bomb you blowed!"

"I didn't blow shit up!" Karbonado said, not denying Checkmate did.

"How the hell did all them bodies end up on yo' property in pieces then? Explain that. Because the police and the city of Houston damn sure wanna know!" J-Money assured him, slamming his hand on the table.

Karbonado shook his head, knowing he was in some shit. He had to admit Checkmate had gone to the extreme.

215

"I can't protect you if I'm blind!" J-Money said. "I understand you not wantin' to speak on what went down in the streets. But you my family, and I'll do everything in my power to protect you. But I need to know the real."

"My girl," Karbonado finally said, "she shot a grenade." He had that nasty little smirk on his face.

"How in the hell she get ahold to some shit like that?" he asked, shocked.

"Same thing I asked. But no matter what, I'm glad she had it 'cause if she didn't, we would most likely be dead. It was too many guns against just the two of us. I thought I was dead, fam," Karbonado explained.

J-Money shook his head because he knew that it was going to be hard trying to cover up Karbonado's mess, but he planned to keep his word and do everything in his power to protect his family.

"I'm gonna need a million by the end of next week. It's a lot of hands I'm gonna have to grease to sweep this under the rug.

*****

Chapter 36

$$$

Weeks later...

"It's all yo' fault!" Karbonado yelled. He had just gotten the news from J-Money that he wasn't going to be able to get them off the hook. J-Money explained that the Feds had gotten involved and they wanted answers for the blown up bodies.

"How the fuck is it my fault?! I saved the mornin', afternoon, day, and night! Fuck you! Don't be tryna put this all on me!" Checkmate responded.

"Bitch, you keep talkin' that gangsta shit. I'mma punch you in yo' mouth, and see if you can save yo' teeth!"

While they were in the middle of their argument, Jania walked through the front door. "What ya'll fightin' 'bout now?"

"Yo' stupid ass Momma about to get us sent to prison!"

"Don't keep sayin' that shit! If I didn't do what I did, then we would be buried right now!"

"What did you do, Momma?"

"She killed a bunch of people by shootin' a missile! Now we both in trouble." Jania looked at her and couldn't find the right question.

"How... where did you get a missile from?"

"Exactly! We been livin' here all this time and notyonce did she tell me she had a bomb in here!" Karbonado continued to speak at the loudest volume : he could.

"Maaan, fuck you, hoe ass nigga! I should of blowed yo' ungrateful ass up!" Checkmate slammed her hand on the kitchen counter. She upset at the fact that everything was coming to an end all because she decided to use self defense. She couldn't accept the fact that she was all the way in the wrong. She turned around and walked to her room, slamming the door so hard that she knocked a picture off the wall causing the glass to shatter. an en

"Daddy, you can't just blame everything on her." "I'm not! But she's the reason we goin' down! And -".

"Daddy, calm down. Ya'll been through worse. How much time are ya'll lookin' at?" she asked in a low caring tone.

"I dont know, but I damn sure wasn't lookin' to do shit!

Matter fact, I'm not about to wait on 'em to come get me," he said then ran from the room. When he got in the bedroom, he told Checkmate, "Baby, get up and pack yo' shit. We about to duck off to Miami. Fuck waitin' on the feds to come get us. If we gotta go down, then let's make 'em do their job." He began packing a bag full of his stuff.

Karbonado called Diamond Dawg and explained his situation, and like a true friend, Diamond Dawg told him to come on down.

He went back out to the living room when he was finished. "Nia, we goin ' to Miami. What you gonna do? You stayin' here with P. or you comin'?" Karbonado asked.

"I'm gonna stay. So y'all gonna hide out there?"

"Yeah, as long as we can. Just make sure nobody know where we went but Lil Moma, Rowdy, P., Damn Fool, and Kaci," he told her with a serious expression on his face.

"Okay, Daddy, y'all be safe. And make sure my brother and sisters keep in touch with me," she said with a smile.

"You know them kids not gonna go a day without blowin' yo' phone up!" Checkmate said, coming out of the bedroom and hugging her daughter.

"Look, make sure you got the kids' stuff packed too. It's time for us to get out of here," Karbonado told Checkmate.

"Yeah, we just gotta pick them up from school and we out," she responded.

They both grabbed all of their bags and took them to the truck. After making sure they got everything, they gave Jania hugs and headed to pick up the kids so they could get out of town.

*****

"My friend!" Diamond Dawg greeted them with excitement as he held the door open for Karbonado and his family to enter his house.

"And who might these pretty little angels be?" he asked with a smile.

"This right here is Diamond. And this is Princess and Lil Daddy," Karbonado told him with pride. "And you already met Checkmate."

"Well, y'all make yourselves comfortable. You can use this house as long as you need."

"Oh, please don't say that! The last time we came for Jania's party, I didn't want to leave this house. Now I come back and you tellin' me I can stay as long as I want? I love this house!" Checkmate said, excited by the house again.

"I'll tell you what," Diamond Dawg said, "this house cost 15.7 million. I'll give it to you, but I need you to put in some work for me." The look on his face told her he was serious.

Checkmate looked at him telling herself, "Here comes some more bullshit." She asked him, "What kind of work you talkin' about?"

"I would like to hire you as my secret assassin. I have a few people that need to be dealt with. Each one of them I'm goin' to give you everything you need to know about them. And—"

"—So you expect me to kill some people just to have this house? Come on, Diamond Dawg, we millionaires too. We can buy a house brand new for that same price."

Diamond Dawg laughed. "Baby girl, this shit is bigger than just the house. I'm offering you more muscle than you already have. I'm offering a lot of property to leave your kids. I'm talking expensive property in Miami and Orlando. I'm talking owning restaurants and clubs out here. All that will come with this house if you take these contracts and complete the mission."

Checkmate thought about everything he was saying and she had to admit he gave her an offer that was hard to turn down, but she wasn't a fool. She knew he could get some of his goons to do the hits. "Why me, though? We both know you run Miami."

"Because I like your style. I like how you move. A lot of these men will underestimate you because you're beautiful. And I know your looks will be the cause of their death. Trust me when I tell you all of this."

"Listen, Diamond Dawg, I respect you because you have opened up doors and allowed me and Karbonado to feed our family. So for that reason, I'm gonna accept these contracts. But I'm askin' you with respect not to fuck with me. When everything's done, I need everything you offered or I promise… you either gonna kill me or I'm gonna kill you," she said, looking him straight in the eye.

Diamond Dawg loved how direct she was with him. He smiled then stuck out his hand to shake on it. "Loyalty and my word is all I live and die by," he said.

She accepted his hand. "And that's the only thing that matters to me."

Diamond Dawg told her he would have everything ready for her in a week. And with nothing else to say, he let her go find the kids and Karbonado.

"Girl, what the fuck wrong with you?" Karbonado asked her when she caught up with them. "We supposed to be layin' low, and you come right down here and accept a contract." He was trying to keep his voice low so that the kids couldn't hear him, but he was pissed.

"Did you hear what he offered? That's why I jumped on it. We might be goin' to the feds, and we don't know for how long. So why not build as much as we can so our kids won't have to depend on nobody? I didn't make the decision for you or me. I'm doin' this for Diamond, Princess, and Lil Daddy, and even Asia. And even though Jania about to get married, I'm gonna make sure she have everything she need too.

"Once the mission complete, then I'm gonna sign all the Miami and Orlando property over to Jania, and she's to make sure the kids are taken care of."

Karbonado had to admit that Checkmate had a very good point, but he was still upset that she wouldn't just sit down. "Damn, baby, you know I'm gonna support you and ride for you, but you playin' some dangerous games," he warned her.

"Yeah, I know. It's call *A Game of Murder*!"

Coming Soon

The Murder of a Boss 2

Checkmate: A Game of Murder

Made in the USA
Coppell, TX
04 December 2023